WAITING ON YOU

A BROOKLYN LOVE STORY

Z. L. ARKADIE

Z.L. ARKADIE BOOKS

ISBN: 978-1-942857-37-2

Robin Hester sort of hated the fact that her cousin Sonja had invited Dexter Frampton to dinner. That was why all night long Robin had been purposely giving him the cold shoulder. Something about him made her want to resist being sucked into his allure. His appearance wasn't the culprit; it was something far deeper.

She had met Dexter two days prior at Jay West's house. Jay and Sonja were writing a TV show together based on their grandmother, Lorraine Hester's, secret past. The two of them were returning from their trip to Texas and would be home at any minute. Robin wanted to be there to confront Sonja as soon as she walked through the door. Sonja and Jay had pulled scars off old wounds without Gran's knowledge. Sonja could be careless in that way. Robin hated the duplicitous nature in which her cousin had operated, but the fact that she had agreed to keep their little mission hush-hush made her just as culpable.

When Robin arrived at Jay's house, it was Dexter who let her past the gates and greeted her at the front door. She was caught off guard by how strikingly attractive he was. At first, she thought he was one of Jay's actor friends. She'd heard Jay would let his loser friends throw explicit parties at his house sometimes. At least that was what his ex-girlfriend, Plume Ashbury, had told her. But when the houseguest said his name, Robin realized the tall, well-built man with piercing blue eyes and honey skin was Sonja's new writing partner. Usually, a man had to be more than good-looking for Robin to give him a second thought. She was reminding herself of that as they sat across from each other in the den, waiting for Sonja and Jay to arrive.

They sat in silence for longer than she was comfortable with. Robin had never been good at small talk, so she was feverishly trying to think of something to say.

"Haven't I seen you somewhere before?" Dexter finally asked.

Robin looked up from her sweaty palms. She'd been trying to focus on everything else in Jay's sparsely decorated and sterile room instead of Dexter's face. The white cabinets, tables, and empty glass vases revealed just how lonely their childhood friend, who'd just recently reconnected with his family, had been for the last fifteen years.

She set her gaze on his alluring smile. "Sorry, what did you say?"

"You look familiar. Do we know each other?"

It took her a moment to stop studying all the perfect lines and angles of his face. She was searching for an imperfection, but there were none. "I don't know. Do we?"

He turned his head slightly to the right. "It's just that you look familiar."

"Well, Sonja and I favor each other, so…"

"No. I'm aware of that." He shook his index finger. "You're Robin Hester. My daughter likes your art."

Robin watched him cross his legs as though he were proud of himself for figuring out the mystery of her identity. However, his face continued to hold her in captivity. She couldn't look away from it no matter how hard she tried. "How old are you?" she blurted.

3

He sat up straight. "How old am I?"

"Yes." There was a sense of desperation in her voice.

He pursed his lips, frowning.

"I'm asking because you look pretty young to have a daughter old enough to appreciate my art."

Then he grinned again. "I thought good art had no restrictions when it came to admiration."

She was trapped in his smoldering gaze and was amazed by how easily aroused she felt in his presence. It usually took a lot more than a sexy face to get her juices flowing, and that was still the case. So it had to have been more than all the variations of his attractive expressions. It was something more that she found so captivating about him, but she still couldn't put her finger on it.

He cleared his throat and adjusted in his seat. "My daughters are—"

Robin jerked her head. "You have more than one?"

He raised two fingers. "I have two."

She frowned, thinking they must be very young or he had exceptional genes.

"Maribel and Mariana. That's their names."

"Humph," she said.

"You don't like kids?"

She realized she was having a conversation with herself and not saying much to him. That was something she did often, which made people believe either she was a snobbish artist or not playing with a full deck.

She shook her head fervently. "I mean, I like kids... for the most part."

"For the most part?"

"It might be quieter when they're not around. But I guess that depends on the kid."

With his arms folded across his chest, Dexter grinned at her as though he were thoroughly amused. "Can I ask you something?"

She groaned woefully. "Please do, especially if you're about to change the subject."

"I am."

"You are?"

"I'm about to change the subject."

Pull it together, Robbie. She sat up straight, composing herself. "I'm all ears."

"So, what made you want to become an artist?"

Robin had a practiced answer for that question, which she had been asked numerous times during her career. But his entrancing blue eyes made her forget it. Or maybe it wasn't the color of his eyes but the way he looked at her that discombobulated her. Or perhaps it was something else—that unidentifiable thing that made her want to experience him in all kinds of ways, especially sexually.

She could feel the tension in her face from frowning. "I don't know."

He looked surprised. "You don't?"

"I guess because painting and drawing has always come easy to me. Then when I'm in it, something speaks." She closed her eyes to feel the emotions soaring through her. "No. It yells, it screams, it says, 'I'm here.' But I can never hear the voice unless I'm creating."

Dexter watched her with his mouth open. Robin felt like hiding inside her skin. She had definitely said too much. Thank God the alarm system announced the rear parking door had opened.

Dexter's blue eyes gleamed at her as though they were saying more than his words could convey.

"Dexter, are you in there?" Jay called.

"We're in the den!" he said.

"We?"

Dexter grinned. "Robin and I."

Finally, Sonja and Jay appeared, and Robin said goodbye to Dexter to have it out with Sonja about nosing around in their grandmother's past.

After leaving Jay's, Robin drove to Mars

MacAvoy's house. Mars was an actor who, for the last two weeks, had been her secret obsession. She went to see him on a whim, hoping that one look at Mars would get Dexter's beautiful blue eyes out of her head.

Mars didn't live that far away from Jay. However, when Robin made it to the security gates of his property and called the house, Lourdes, his housekeeper, said he wasn't home and would be gone for a week on business.

Robin frowned. "Funny, I spoke with him this morning, and he never mentioned that to me."

"Oh, I don't know," Lourdes replied. "That's what I know."

Robin could hear the frustration in Lourdes's tone. She'd only met the woman twice, and the way Lourdes avoided looking at her face was a clue that the housekeeper knew Mars was involved with other women and loyal to none. But Robin already knew that and didn't care. When they had sex, Mars had an intoxicating way of making her feel as if she were the most desirable woman on earth, not loved or cherished, but desired. Although as soon as their sex ended and he came, there was never any petting, cuddling, or pillow talk. He would make up an excuse to get away from her as fast as he could.

He was no good for her or any other woman. She knew Mars couldn't be changed; he was too messed up in the brain to change. It had been two days since she'd driven away from Mars's gates, and she still hadn't heard from him.

Before arriving at her cousin Elaine's house for dinner that evening, she had forgotten about Dexter Frampton and his intoxicating energy. Throughout the evening, every time her eyes found his baby blues, they were already watching her. More than a few times, his smoldering stare made her thighs quiver. There was something about Dexter that was different from Mars. She was quite certain Frampton wasn't a love-them-and leave-them type of guy. Robin had never had one of those kinds of guys before. The men she chose to get involved with had the sort of mommy issues that made them impossible to take seriously, and that went for Mars too.

Dexter Frampton was the real deal—the sexy, smart, and more importantly, healthy real deal. Mars was junk food, and Dexter was a Michelin-star four-course meal.

Dinner ended minutes after midnight. Robin lingered to use the bathroom. She'd had two glasses of wine then two cups of coffee, and all the liquid had gone right through her. By the time she was done in the bathroom, everyone but one person had already left. As she walked down the hallway to the front door, she could feel a presence behind her. Robin stopped. She knew it was Dexter. Her heart pounded like crazy. She closed her eyes in an attempt to silence the voice inside her that was telling her not to deny this man the pleasure of having his way with her. In that moment of complete honesty, she inhaled deeply, held the air, then pushed it out of her lungs. Robin whipped herself around.

There was something wildly lustful in Dexter's pale-blue eyes as he continued taking deliberate steps toward her. Then their mouths crashed into each other. His soft, warm tongue eagerly swirled around hers.

"Let's get out of here," Robin whispered, taking his hand and guiding him. She made it two steps before he tugged her against him then pressed her against the wall and kissed her deeply.

Robin's head spun like a top. Her panties were drenched, and her pussy throbbed for more. It felt as if her body would explode if he didn't take her right there and then.

"Let's stay here," he said, searching over both

shoulders for anyone else who might be around. "I want you now."

"Me too," she said breathlessly.

"Well then, stay at your house. I don't care," Elaine said loudly. She wasn't in sight, but the sound of her footsteps was getting closer.

"I have a morning meeting in downtown LA. I don't want to fuck with PCH and the 10 Freeway in the morning," Gary, Elaine's fiancé, whined.

"You said that already. Three times. Why do you feel the need to say it again? Are you lying?"

"Jeez, Laney. I can't fucking win with you."

Robin and Dexter stepped away from each other and made themselves appear cool, calm, and collected as the bickering couple rounded the corner.

Elaine halted, glowering at them as if they had stolen the silverware. "Robin? You're still here?"

Robin could feel her eyes expand. "Um, we were just talking, Dexter and I."

Elaine bolted toward them. "Well, you have to go now because I'm setting the alarm."

Robin knew her cousin well enough to know that Elaine was embarrassed that she and Dexter had heard the couple arguing. The more Elaine tried to make it appear as if she and Gary had a healthy relationship, the more evidence she provided to the contrary. However, Robin took Elaine's interruption as a sign from above.

"Got it. Good night." Robin made a mad dash toward the front door and didn't stop as the warm August night gushed across her face.

"Robin," Dexter called. "Robin," he said louder.

She pressed the button to remotely unlock her car then stood by the driver's door. Her eyes closed tightly when she felt Dexter's presence wash over her. "That was…" She cleared her throat. "We were about to make a mistake."

His hand massaged her shoulder, sending a surge of desire racing through her. "That didn't feel like a mistake to me," he said.

She refused to turn and look at him. If she did that, then she would lose all her will to resist him. "I just can't."

"You can't?" He sounded disappointed.

"No," she whispered and immediately wanted to take it back.

He must've stepped away from her because Robin could no longer feel him near.

"Okay," he said. "How about dinner tomorrow night? I could…"

Robin squeezed her eyes tighter. "No. I can't."

"Why not?"

"I just can't." She swung her car door open.

"Wait a minute. Are you saying I have no chance here?"

A picture of Mars came into mind and remained with her as she finally faced Dexter. His face caused her to skip a breath. Looking at him made her picture shit that always terrified her, like love, loyalty, and happily ever after. Her mother was the worst at being in a stable relationship with a really good guy. Robin was certain her mother's bad habits had rubbed off on her. She would ruin everything that was good about Dexter Frampton. He would end up hating her. Not only was he Sonja's writing partner, but he was Elaine's client. No matter what, he was going to be in Robin's life long after she gave into her lust, made mad, passionate love to him, and broke his heart. She would rather exist with him in peace than in enmity.

"No, I'm not saying that." She groaned as she sighed. "Let's start slower than having dinner tomorrow night. Plus, aren't you flying to Vancouver in the morning?"

He blew his cheeks out and released the air. "Ah

shit, I forgot." He folded his arms. "But I'm curious. How do you start slower than dinner? Coffee?"

She snorted at his astute comeback. "How about I call you sometime? We'll talk and get to know each other better."

He tilted his head slightly. "On the phone?"

"Or text."

He rubbed the side of his head. "If you're not into me, Robin, then say it. Don't bullshit me."

She could look in his eyes and tell that he'd been hurt before. All she had to say was, "I'm seeing someone else, and our timing is off. That's all." But that wouldn't have been the whole truth. She was seeing someone, but their timing wasn't off. She was just scared as hell of him.

"Let's just be friends, cordial," she said.

"I see." He studied her. "I'll call you sometime. How about that?"

She sighed with relief and nodded.

They exchanged numbers then parted ways. As Robin drove back to her apartment complex, which she currently managed, she was struck by inspiration. It had been so long since she'd had some artistic vision. She'd lost count of how many months she had been creatively blocked. Everything she painted was utter shit. But an installation had come to mind. She saw lights blasting out of her heart. She saw those particles split and become matter. The vision was calling her, asking her to please make it real. So instead of heading home, she went in the opposite direction. Tonight, she would head to her Venice Beach studio and create what her heart could not deny.

CHAPTER 1

ONE YEAR LATER

*R*obin Hester frantically brushed on mascara and dropped the tube back in the overnight case she'd been living out of for the past three weeks while in New York City. She was going to be late to her own art exhibit, which really pissed her off. Her gran had always taught her to be prompt to even the smallest affair, and that night was big. She would be showing her light installations to the public for the first time.

Mars, her date for the evening, was supposed to have swung by and picked her up a half hour ago. But he'd called at the last minute to say he would meet her at the venue. He'd given no explanation for his sudden change of plan and had ended their call before she could ask for one.

Her cell phone rang again, and she knew it was either Claudia François, her new manager; Sonja calling from Vancouver to wish her good luck; Elaine calling from LA to remind her to own her success and not to let them see her sweat; Theresa calling from Seattle to say she wished she could be there; or the taxi service.

After looking at the face of her device, she answered it. "Hi, I'm on my way down."

The service rep for the cab company thanked her.

Robin sighed after taking one last look at herself in the mirror. Makeup was never her friend. It always made her look like a seven-year-old pageant queen. With only seconds to spare, she grabbed her tube of facial cleanser and washed her face.

"There," she said after towel drying her skin. She felt like herself again, almost. Claudia had convinced her to wear a long black dress, which made her look like Elvira, Mistress of the Dark, from the neck down. If only she had enough time to change into her black pants and white T-shirt. She fought the urge to do just that and instead grabbed her small purse and headed out.

Claudia called again while Robin was in the taxi then texted "911" when she didn't answer. It was always an emergency with her, though. Robin was well aware that she was forty minutes late, and she didn't want Claudia making her feel guilty about it.

As she stuffed her cell phone back into her purse, she paid special attention to her shaky hands. Robin took a few deep breaths. Her nerves were through the roof. She had just completed her first installation light show. She had spent most of the year locked away in her Venice Beach studio, figuring out how to make wire, lights, plastic, and other reflective material bend to her will. Instead of showing in LA, Claudia had convinced her to hold her exhibition in New York City, which was something Robin had never done. Her first showings had always been held in her hometown. LA was where she felt the most comfortable, which was what she had conveyed to Claudia.

"But why?" Claudia had asked in a French accent that came and went at will.

"Because it's home," she had said.

"But New York is New York. If you make it there, then you can make it anywhere. There's no saying like that about LA. And there are reasons why."

Robin rolled her eyes. "I understand those

reasons. One deep look at the city holds the answers. It's gritty, dirty, overpopulated…"

Claudia took her by the shoulders. "It also has the Temperance Gallery." She flexed her eyebrows twice as she grinned from ear to ear.

Robin pressed her lips together and widened her eyes as a question raced through her head.

Claudia smiled proudly. "Yes, you're in. I got you in."

Robin had done something she'd never done before. She had screamed, jumped up and down, and even cried.

The Temperance Gallery was a six-floor town-house on Manhattan's Upper East Side. It was once the residence of Temperance Pope, a famous female art dealer in the early to mid-twentieth century. She'd lived alone. When she died, her body was found in the basement, resting in a casket she had purchased for herself and surrounded by never-before-seen paintings from a number of the world's greatest artists like Picasso, Frida Kahlo, Salvador Dali, Jackson Pollock, more vaginas by Georgia O'Keeffe, and many others. On top of her body was a letter asking her best friend Nora Kaufman to auction the paintings and use the proceeds to allow her abode to continue being the home for the works of those great artists that would come after her. Since the death of Temperance Pope in 1956, only 127 living artists had shown at the gallery that was once her house. Robin was excited and terrified to be number 128, and that was why she was shaking like a leaf in the wind.

"Ma'am, we're here, but this is as close as I can get you," the driver said.

She looked up from her shivering hands and out the windshield. Her jaw dropped. Up ahead, chauffeured limousines and Escalades with tinted windows were piled up, one behind the other, in front of the gallery. Taxi drivers were honking at each other, trying to get closer or pass other cars. A line had formed at the steps of the Temperance Gallery that went all the way down Seventy-Fourth Street and curved around onto Fifth Avenue. A red carpet running down the front steps glistened under spotlights. And to top off the spectacle, paparazzi stood at the iron gates, snapping pictures. If Claudia had planned the night to unfold in such a way, she'd never told Robin anything about it. Robin would have no doubt pushed back against Claudia's grand scheme. She didn't need the hoopla and sure as hell didn't want it. Claudia insisting that she dress like Elvira and wear a truckload of makeup suddenly made sense.

The driver exaggerated clearing his throat. "Ma'am, what are you going to do?"

"Oh, um…" Robin frowned, deliberating on whether or not she should instruct the driver to take her back to the hotel. She didn't want any part of the bloated event. She would rather read about what everyone thought the next day in the paper than face a bunch of amateur art enthusiasts who wouldn't get what she was trying to convey.

But what was she trying to convey?

Knock, knock, knock.

Robin jumped and turned quickly to the rear driver's side window. Mars's movie-star handsome face was near the glass, and he was waving at her.

MARS PAID THE DRIVER AND, AS USUAL, DIDN'T TIP —he only did that when an attractive waitress was involved.

"Really, no tip?" Robin scolded with narrowed eyes.

He swept his arm around her waist and started

guiding her up the sidewalk. "No. We're late. Let's go."

She ripped herself out of Mars's grasp and knocked on the driver's window before he could flee the scene. She dug in her wallet and tipped him twenty bucks.

"Hey, is that Mars MacAvoy?" the driver asked.

She was tempted to lie out of sheer embarrassment. "Yeah, it's him."

"What a cheap asshole."

Robin agreed. She could always count on Mars MacAvoy to be a dick. He was entitled and arrogant, even if he was one of the greatest actors in the world. Plus his dark hair, emerald-green eyes, and facial features, which made him pretty but manly, gave him serious beauty capital.

"Sorry about that," she said and slammed the door.

At first, Mars refused to take her hand. She knew he was upset that she had tipped the driver. It was something she did often—compensate for his shortcomings—and as usual, she felt uncomfortable about it.

But he gripped her hand once they were in the lenses of cameras and the flashing lights were bouncing off them. "You know they get paid a salary, right?"

"Who?" she asked.

Mars was wearing his obligatory fake actor's smile. "The cabbie."

She rolled her eyes. "I don't want to argue about your lack of generosity tonight."

Someone called Mars's name. Lights flashed, blinding Robin.

"Fuck it. Just smile," he said coldly while still smiling.

Robin couldn't fake it, so she didn't.

"It's her, Robin Hester!" a young girl's voice said as they swept past the line.

The fact that it was late and she heard a child's voice made Robin scowl in the direction of the speaker. She was even more pissed at Claudia. What had her manager been thinking? She wasn't doing Disneyland art. Her work was deep, emotional, and thought-provoking. Robin's glare met the beaming face of a girl who was probably eleven or twelve years old. There was something familiar about her pale-blue eyes. Then she looked up at the older gentleman who had his hands planted protectively on the girl's shoulders.

Now she remembered where she'd seen those eyes before. Robin stopped abruptly. "Dexter?"

Dexter smiled broadly until his pale-blue eyes focused on Mars's arm around her waist. "Robin," he said frostily.

She closed her mouth and swallowed then asked, "What are you doing here?"

He scowled at Mars again. "We're here to see the show."

Mars drew Robin closer against him and whispered, "We have to keep moving."

Robin huffed as she scowled at her late and rude date and focused back on Dexter and his daughter. "You said you had two daughters. Mariana and Maribel."

His eyes lit up. "You remembered?"

Robin smiled faintly as she nodded. Of course she remembered. She'd been trying hard to forget everything about Dexter Frampton, but he had always made that hard by showing up unexpectedly in her life.

Dexter's manly hands massaged the beaming girl's tiny shoulders. "Yes, this is Mariana, my youngest. I told you she was a fan."

"Yes, I remember."

It felt as though they were caught in the lights of the flashing cameras.

"Dexter Frampton, right?" Mars asked extra loudly.

Robin cringed at Mars's condescending tone. It was his way of establishing hierarchies—he was a world-famous actor, and Dexter wasn't in his league.

"That's a good memory you have there, Mars. I'm surprised since I'm one of the little people," Dexter said.

Mars snarled as he grunted bitterly.

"You two know each other?" Robin asked, curious to find out what was behind the animosity between them.

"She's here!" Claudia called out. "Robin Hester has arrived!"

People standing in line started clapping. Those who were walking down the steps, taking the exit lane, were cheering too.

"Congratulations," the woman in front of Mariana said excitedly with her hands pressed in prayer on her chest.

The flashing lights really started blinding her. When she noticed Mariana squinting as though the glares were hurting her eyes, Robin was just about to invite Dexter and his daughter to walk in with them. But Mars dragged her away so fast that she couldn't go back without causing a scene. She felt horrible about leaving Dexter and Mariana in line. First of all, she wasn't quite ready to leave his presence. Perhaps it was because his face stirred within her the same state of confusion seeing him always caused. Robin wanted to figure out why his mere presence equally drew her in and repelled her. Plus, if Sonja or Elaine discovered she had left him in line on such a smoldering August night, they would scold her for not being gracious to family friends.

Her mind was still on Dexter as Claudia took her by the shoulders and put a gentle kiss on both of her cheeks. Claudia wore a slinky red gown that made her look like a striking beauty, especially with the contrast of her raven hair cascading past her breasts. She smelled like strawberry lip gloss. The mayhem couldn't hide the way Mars was eye-banging her. But he did that often to other women. It used to irritate the hell out of Robin, but he'd managed to convince her that he was merely a man who admired beauty in people, places, and things. Robin could respect that. After all, she was an artist who also had an eye for exotic and beautiful people, places, and things. And that night, Claudia was a vision to behold.

"Why are you so late?" Claudia asked through her painted-on smile.

"I'm sorry," Robin said. "Um, Mars—"

"Mars?" Claudia scowled at him. "It's always about you, isn't it?"

He jutted his chin out at her. "I'm doing you a fucking favor. Don't forget it."

"I'm sure you won't let me."

Robin shook her head in disbelief. "What does he mean by doing you a favor?"

"Star presence, darling. That's why we need him here. But that's it, and that's all." Claudia flopped a hand dismissively as she broadened her fake smile. "You can go now," she said to Mars. "Your job is over."

Robin's eyes scaled over the long line of people waiting to experience her exhibit. However, her gaze stopped cold on Dexter, who was staring at her. Her heart skipped a beat. "Did you pay all these people to be here?"

Claudia linked arms with her and guided her the rest of the way up the steps. "We paid for the press, the early viewings, and appearances by some major public figures who were already fans of your art to make this event a success, which it is, and you're welcome."

They entered the gallery and rushed down the small hallway and past the stairs that led to the exhibit floor upstairs.

"Press is waiting for you," Claudia said. "They're getting antsy, but none of them will dare leave."

Robin couldn't get the picture of Dexter and Mariana standing in the humid night out of her head.

The sound of Claudia's heels clicking against the white marble floor echoed above the rumble of voices resonating from the stairwell they had just passed. The voices all sounded excited, but she also thought she heard whimpering.

"When you meet the press, be charming." Claudia raised her eyebrows at Robin. "Do you remember our lessons?"

Robin stopped walking. "Claudia, I need you to do something for me first."

"Don't stop. Keep walking," Claudia whined, still trying to drag her along.

Robin planted her feet. "The press can wait, and yes, I can be charming. But I need you to go out there and find a guy standing in line with his little girl and bring them in."

"That's almost like searching for a needle in a haystack."

"Not really, but they both have the sort of striking blue eyes that'll separate them from the rest."

Claudia sighed briskly, clearly agitated.

"I'll walk into that pressroom and charm their asses off if you go out there"—Robin pointed toward the entrance—"find Dexter Frampton and his daughter Mariana, bring them in, and give them VIP treatment. Got it?"

Claudia frowned as if she were having a hard time keeping up. "Who's Dexter Frampton?"

"Man with blue eyes. Little girl with blue eyes."

"There are a lot of people with blue eyes out there."

"Not like theirs. And if that's not enough, then ask Mars. He knows him."

"Claudia, they're getting restless," Ronnie, one of Claudia's assistants, called while trying to control her volume from up the hallway. She was standing in the doorway of the pressroom.

Claudia pushed Robin toward Ronnie. "Okay, I'll find this Dennis. Just go."

Robin shook her head, fearing Claudia would not be able to complete the task. "It's Dexter."

"Okay, I'll find him."

Robin hesitated.

"And I'll give the man and little girl with the blue eyes the VIP treatment. Just go."

That made Robin feel slightly more confident in Claudia. So without further delay, she raised her thumb then went into the media room to engage in what she'd always considered the worst part of opening night.

"So what was your inspiration?" Krista Lambert asked. She was a spritely local reporter with over-bleached blond hair cut into a perfect bob. "And don't give me the same bullshit answer you gave the others."

Robin felt as if she had been in the small room forever. The flow of reporters and columnists was nonstop. Krista was her sixth or seventh interview, and others were waiting in the wings, eager to get their time alone with her. One thing had become glaringly clear to Robin—her exhibit was a big hit, bigger than she could've ever imagined. The crowd moving into the gallery was composed of genuine art enthusiasts.

"Oh, I see," Krista said, visibly reading Robin's expression.

Robin tilted her head slightly. "You see what?"

"You don't quite understand the effect your installations are having on people, do you?"

Robin frowned.

"Have you been in the exhibit room since you've arrived?"

"No. I haven't."

"You should go take a look."

Robin grimaced.

Krista leaned closer and lowered her voice. "Because if you don't know what you did to elicit such a response, then we have no faith that you'll be able to repeat the same results in the future." She sat up. "And you don't want us to think that."

THE EXHIBIT ROOM SPANNED THE ENTIRE SECOND floor, which was over three thousand square feet. Robin had spent weeks setting up the exhibit with four art students from NYU. Each had signed a nondisclosure statement to keep the installation project secret. Just before Robin walked into the exhibit, she passed more people who were wiping their eyes and sniffing.

She frowned. She had heard crying earlier. *Why are people crying?*

A couple walked past her, kissing as if they couldn't keep their lips off each other. Others passed her, smiling and giggling. Then there were more criers. They were all so wrapped up in their emotions that they didn't even notice her standing there, which was a stark difference from being outside, where everyone had been calling her name.

Without further delay, Robin walked into her exhibit.

CHAPTER 2

DEXTER FRAMPTON

Two Hours Ago

*D*exter tried not to show Mariana how livid he was. Of all the assholes in the world, Robin Hester had chosen Mars MacAvoy to keep her company. He would've done anything for her if she had chosen him. He was a good guy. Mars was not. At least he knew why she'd rejected him at every turn.

He had last seen her at Elaine and Zach Lord's strange shindig. She had mentioned she'd been locked in her studio, finishing up a project. When others at their table pressed her for more details, she was typically aloof about answering their questions.

Something about her demeanor irritated the hell out of Dexter.

"Why so secretive?" he asked.

"I'm not being secretive," she said in a lackluster tone without looking him in the eyes.

He felt his lips snarl. "I get that this is your usual disposition, but I'm sure you have more speeds than being aloof hidden somewhere in there."

Finally, she glared up at him. "Of course I do. But perhaps you haven't inspired more out of me than what you get."

It was a great comeback, and he cracked a smile. They had gone at it that way all night long until she'd announced she had to leave.

The problem was he could never forget that kiss they'd shared in Elaine's hallway. Deep down, Dexter believed that every time he came in contact with Robin Hester and didn't leave with her heart securely in his hands, he was doing his soul a disservice. Well, he *had* felt that way until tonight. The way Mars's hand had grasped her waist... His touch was too intimate. *They've had sex.*

Fuck her.

"Dad, are you okay?" Mariana asked.

Suddenly, he realized he'd been squeezing his eyes shut, attempting to banish last year's kiss between him and Robin from his mind. "Yeah, I am, sweetie."

"But Dad, why are people crying?" Mariana asked.

"Crying?" Dexter hadn't noticed how close they'd moved to the front of the line. His mind had been too occupied with the night's artist. But Mariana was right. Some people walking out of the building were wiping their eyes as they headed up or down the street. He grunted curiously. "I don't know why they're crying."

That was when Dexter glimpsed a woman walking in his direction, grinning at him. He recognized her as the person who'd kissed Robin on both cheeks earlier before pulling her into the gallery.

The woman smiled as she stopped in front of him. "You're Dennis Frampton, are you not?" She had an accent, which sounded French with a touch of British English and Australian.

"I'm Dexter Frampton."

"Oh." Her smile expanded. "I apologize."

"No apology necessary," he said.

She stared at him without saying anything.

"Can I help you with something?" he asked.

"Oh." Her hand flew up and touched her collarbone as she shook her head. "I'm Claudia,

Robin's manager, and I'll give you the VIP treatment. Robin insisted."

He was shocked to hear that. "She did?"

"Yes. But now, *I* insist on giving you the VIP treatment." She was definitely flirting.

Then it finally occurred to him that Robin was merely having a Hester girl reaction to him being there. They were all mindful of one another's friends. If Sonja were to find out that Robin had left Dexter standing in line with Mariana, she would plow into her for being discourteous. So it wasn't personal. Robin was just covering her ass.

Dexter looked down at his daughter. "Are you in, Mari?"

Mariana's face brightened. "Am I going to meet Robin Hester again?"

"Not tonight, darling." Claudia's smoldering gaze made Dexter feel like prime rib on bone china. "Robin's in press, but I'll be your personal escort."

Mariana smiled, but it wasn't genuine. She was used to women hitting on him, and she didn't like it. Regardless, Dexter and Luddie, his ex-wife, had taught their children to be respectful always, and that was the expression Mariana was showing—the polite one.

"Then follow me," Claudia sang, making sure

she walked beside him and not in front of him. "So tell me about yourself, Dexter."

Before he could answer, people started clapping at the arrival of Jessica St. James, an eccentric pop star who'd recently ventured into acting. She had auditioned for a part in *Pact of Lies* two days ago. Vince, the president of the production company that produced their TV show, had asked that Dexter and Sonja strongly consider her for a role. St. James would boost their already record-breaking ratings and give them a new demographic to pitch to advertisers.

That was one of many things Dexter liked about Vincent Adams—the man was honest about what was important to him. However, Vince had also said that if Jessica was a terrible actress, then Dexter should feel free to pass.

Jessica was not a great actress, but she wasn't terrible either. She had, however, crossed the line when she'd trapped him in the men's restroom after her audition and offered him a blow job.

"Whoa," Dexter said, pushing her hand away from his crotch. He was still urinating, and his dick was out. "Get the hell out of here."

Her lip curled, showing teeth, but she didn't move an inch.

He angled the front of his body away from her and pointed toward the door with his unoccupied hand. "Get out now!"

"I know all about you," Jessica said like a woman scorned.

Dexter frowned. "Fine. Now get the hell out."

"I know your secret, and if I don't get this job, it's coming out." That was the last thing she'd said before spinning around and storming out.

Now Jessica was posing for the cameras, and the crowd was going mad. Her manufactured expression of glee met Dexter's glare. Then she smirked.

Dexter only had one secret, which he'd carried most of his life. *Does she really know it?*

No one knew the truth other than those involved. Not even his ex-wife, Luddie, or his daughters knew. There was no way Jessica could've found out. *No way.* She was bluffing.

"Do you know Jessica?" Claudia asked.

Dexter held Mariana's hand tighter. That secret would change his and his daughters' lives forever. When he ripped his scowl away from Jessica and faced Claudia, she was leaning away from him, wearing a curious frown. "No, I don't know her."

"Then she would be transfixed by your hotness."

Dexter turned away from Claudia, who was batting her eyelashes. The evening couldn't get worse—could it?

Three Hours Later

CLAUDIA INVITED HIM TO THE AFTER-PARTY. IT WAS for adults only, so he took Mariana to her mother's house, which was the plan anyway. He was scheduled to fly to Vancouver the next day for the start of production on season two of *Pact of Lies*. He was vice president of original content at Adams Entertainment Enterprise, but since he and Sonja had worked together so closely in writing the first season of the series, he'd agreed to spend a couple of weeks with her during production of the second season.

Dexter was gearing up for two weeks of at least sixteen-hour workdays. Sleep would be a special commodity. However, he would've rather been exactly where he was than at home in bed. Even though he'd written Robin off after watching her with Mars, he still wanted to see her, even if it was just to congratulate her. Then he could leave.

The party was being held on the glass-topped terrace of Rush, a new restaurant by celebrity Chef Douglas Nederland in Greenpoint, Brooklyn, which wasn't far from where Dexter lived. Claudia had stuck to him like glue the moment he'd walked through the door.

"Dexter, you made it," she sang as if they were old friends.

He let her kiss both cheeks as his eyes roamed the space, searching for that one person.

Claudia took him by the hand. "Come, have a drink with me." She pulled him along, and he went freely only because he thought she would lead him to Robin.

The event was well attended. He recognized a number of celebrities and people who were decision-makers in the entertainment business.

"I didn't know you were vice president of original content at AEE," Claudia said once they stopped in front of the bar. She raised a hand, and the bartender came over immediately. "Let's see…" She studied Dexter with one eye narrowed. "Vodka on the rocks?"

He cracked a tiny smile. "Bourbon, straight up."

"Oh…" she purred. "You surprise me. I like it."

It wasn't that he didn't find Claudia attractive

and mildly interesting. He just wasn't into her. Dexter turned to face the openness of the room, contemplating a way to let Claudia down gently, and that was when he saw her. Robin was standing along the edge of the terrace, staring out at the Manhattan skyline. Mars was next to her. They were close. He was saying something, and she was stiff.

"So, vice president at AEE. That's a big deal," Claudia said.

Dexter kept his eyes on Robin's sexy backside. "It's less of a big deal and more a job, one that I like." He watched Mars touch the small of Robin's back then cross the floor as though he couldn't get away from her fast enough.

"You're modest too. That's sexy of you."

He shrugged indifferently. "Sexy is in the eye of the beholder."

Robin finally turned to face the room. Her eyes looked sad. That pissed Dexter off. He wasn't mad because Mars had hurt her, but the fact that the jerk had the power to do it made him angry.

When Robin's eyes landed on his face, he quickly turned toward Claudia, purposely ignoring Robin. "Why don't you tell me what made you want to manage artists?"

"Well, my father was also an artist, but he would imitate some of the world's most famous art pieces and then switch them out for the original."

Dexter jerked his head in shock. "So he was an art thief?"

Claudia flexed her eyebrows. "Yes, he was."

Dexter struggled to maintain direct eye contact with Claudia as she talked about her father's career as an art thief. Through his peripheral vision, he could see an interchange of people stepping up to engage Robin in conversation. The bartender served their drinks while Claudia told Dexter how her father was arrested for his crimes and spent fifteen years in a French prison. But before then, she had grown up in a house with some of the most famous portraits the world had ever known hanging on the wall. He thought she'd said the original Mona Lisa was hanging over their fireplace for the better part of two years, but he became too distracted when another guy stepped up to talk to Robin. The guy was too close for Dexter's comfort, then he said something that made Robin chuckle.

"You're into her, aren't you?" Claudia asked.

Dexter flinched. "What?"

"You're not doing a very good job of keeping

your eyes off her. I see you trying, but it's not working."

He sighed with dread. "I'm sorry. I…"

She raised a hand. "Don't apologize. Robin's beautiful and interesting. Hell, if I were a man, I'd be chasing her too." She narrowed her eyes at Robin as she took a gulp of her vodka on the rocks. "Unfortunately, Robin has the worst taste in men, evident by how you're standing here salivating over her and she's sulking over Mars MacAvoy. He's been playing mind games with her ever since I've known them to be together."

"That sounds like him."

"Oh," she said, taken aback. "You know him?"

He told her the story of how Mars was the actor on the first major film he'd ever worked on. "He was a dick to the crew."

"Yes, that's his reputation," Claudia said.

"I caught him coming on to one of his co-stars, Sandy Deleon."

Claudia threw her hands up excitedly. "Yes, her. She starred in *Under the Chimney* with him."

"Yeah, I worked on that film, but you don't see my name in the credits because he got me fired."

"Sandy Deleon was very young in that movie."

"Underage, and he was trying to fuck her. I told

him if he didn't back off, I was going to report him to the authorities."

Claudia's mouth fell open, then she grunted. "You obviously didn't know how the Hollywood game was played."

"I knew how the game was played. I choose to not participate."

She tilted her head slightly. "Is that so?"

He nodded confidently. "That is so."

"Then what makes you so special? Is your father Steven Spielberg?"

That question roused something in him. He stood straight, and his gaze found Jessica St. James, who was busy taking selfies with Tim Hunter, a professional baseball player. The chick was always working. Everything she did was to pad her career. Suddenly, the fact that she might know his secret began to worry him.

"Oh my God!" Claudia exclaimed. When he turned, her expression was wide with excitement. "Is Spielberg your father?"

"No," he said emphatically.

Claudia was digging too deep into the things he liked to keep personal. So he excused himself to do what he'd been avoiding all night.

CHAPTER 3

*R*obin couldn't move a muscle as she watched Dexter approach her. For the last half hour, she'd tried not paying attention to how he flirted shamelessly with Claudia as though it were supposed to make her jealous. It had, but that still didn't change how she felt about him. The idea of being with him in real life scared the hell out of her. However, when Krista Robins had asked what her inspiration was, Dexter's eyes came to mind. So she wondered if several layers beneath her surface, she'd never stopped being infatuated by him.

Now they were face-to-face. He smelled liked citrus and a hint of mint. He always smelled good.

Dexter grinned. "Hi."

She was sure she was smiling too, feeling

relieved that he was standing in front of her and not across the room. "Hi."

"Congratulations on your exhibition. It was moving."

She worked like hell to maintain her composure. "Thank you."

"No, really. I've never seen anything like it."

Robin nodded, and silence fell between them.

"So," they said at the same time.

She smiled and gestured to Dexter, giving him the floor.

"No, you," he said.

Robin wanted to say, "I insist," but after the night's success and not seeing him for such a long time, she decided against it. "I was going to ask how you have been."

"I've been well. And yourself?"

"Busy but well," she replied.

"You look well."

"So do you."

She wanted to kiss him. She couldn't kiss him. But oh, the last time they had kissed… She absent-mindedly slid her fingers across her bottom lip, and he watched her do it.

Dexter cleared his throat. "I expected to see more Hester girls present."

She simpered. "They're all indisposed tonight, but they sent me their best."

"I bet they did."

She and Dexter smiled at each other warmly. Soon, they were gazing into each other's eyes, so she stared at her feet.

"So Mars, huh?" he asked.

Robin looked up. "Mars?"

"You're seeing him?"

She shrugged gently. "I guess. You seem to know him."

"I do."

She waited for him to reveal the nature of their association, but it soon became clear that he wasn't going to say anything.

"You're not going to tell me," she finally said with a smirk.

He smirked back. "Why do you want to know?"

"Why can't you just tell me?"

"I'm sure he has to be a good guy to catch your eye."

"Not so," she said, realizing they had moved closer.

"Ah, I see. You're a masochist when it comes to relationships."

Robin was trapped in his gaze. The fact that he

associated Mars with her being a masochist meant that he knew what sort of asshole Mars could be.

Suddenly, the smell of expensive perfume and rambunctious energy overtook them. "The woman who's all over my walls and the man who's going to give me my next job."

Jessica St. James, who looked as though she'd had way too many drinks, put her arm around Robin's waist as if they were old friends. They were not. Claudia had introduced Jessica to her work. Jessica hadn't been able to resist Claudia's pitch when she'd run down the list of A-list celebrities who had Robin's artwork displayed on their walls.

However, Robin couldn't help but notice the look on Dexter's face. She had never seen it before. It was pure disdain.

"Robin, congratulations. I wish you the best." Dexter's tone was formal.

Her heart sank. He was leaving.

Jessica's eyes focused on Dexter. "I'll see you on set after you call my agent. You have until tomorrow morning, eight a.m. Eastern Standard Time." She looked and sounded sober when she said that.

"Good night, Robin," Dexter said before calmly turning away.

Jessica turned her attention back to Robin. "I just wanted to tell you your show was so fucking fantastic."

Robin ripped her curious gaze off of Dexter's back and set her frown on Jessica. "What the hell was that about?"

Jessica looked totally oblivious to the fact that she had just threatened Dexter. "What was what about?"

Robin turned toward where she'd last seen Dexter. He was gone. Jessica kept talking, but Robin tuned her out. *It's now or never.* The lust that Dexter's presence stirred in her was spilling over.

"Excuse me," she said and noticed most eyes on her as she scrambled across the room. Once she made it to the hallway, a sense of relief overcame her when she saw Dexter standing in front of an elevator that had just opened.

"Dexter," she called.

They locked eyes.

She rushed toward him, although it felt as if she were moving in slow motion. He wrapped his arms around her and drew her into the elevator. The freedom of knowing they were alone and that anything could happen raced through her. Her breaths deepened, and her thighs quivered as they stared into each other's eyes.

"What do you want from me, Robin?" he asked.

Throwing caution to the wind, she pressed her lips against his. His warm and eager mouth quickly took charge. His erection pressed against the top of her pubic bone, grinding against her in unison with his tongue. Her heartbeat sped up. She was so hot. She felt intoxicated, even though she hadn't had a drop of alcohol.

His lips and tongue abandoned hers. "What do you want, Robin?" he whispered thickly.

"I want you. For the night. Could you give me that?"

He was ready. His erection said so.

Dexter frowned. That one look said it all. She was prepared for him to turn her down. Then, instead of returning to her party, she would go back to the hotel, pack, and take the first flight out of New York.

The elevator doors opened. Dexter remained silent as he took her by the hand. Her insides felt as though they would burst. She let him lead her through the restaurant and out the door. It felt as if they were the only two people in the world when he stopped under the dark awning of an already closed bakery. He tugged her against him. His hard chest pressing against her soft breasts felt erotic. They kissed feverishly again.

"Shit," he whispered, shivering from desire.

He led her up the avenue. They didn't speak, although he stopped to kiss her two more times before they reached the steps of his townhouse. Robin easily followed as he unlocked the door, letting them into his home. Normally, she would have taken in the décor, assessing his taste. But they were both too eager to experience each other.

DEXTER LOCKED THE DOOR BEHIND THEM AND quickly faced Robin. His impatient fingers lifted the hem of her dress. His teeth nibbled on her hard nipples, which poked through the material of the dress, as his fingers ventured through the wetness between her legs.

She gasped as he slid his fingers in and out of her pussy. Then his mouth found hers again. Oh, the pleasure... He kissed her deeper, deeper... Then all of a sudden, he stopped kissing her. The blue of his eyes seemed to glow in the dusky room. Robin continued to hold on to Dexter Frampton tightly, never wanting to let him go, even though she would soon have to.

He didn't say a word as their breaths collided. His fingers abandoned her wetness, and the hem of her dress dropped around her ankles. "Should I call you a cab?" he whispered.

Robin pressed her lips together. No, he shouldn't. She wanted him to fuck her brains out. He was on the verge of making love to her like no one else had ever done, not even Mars, who was masterful at fucking.

"Why?" She sounded so disappointed.

"Are you willing to give me all of you?"

"Yes."

"I mean all of you. I don't want us to end after I make love to you."

Now she understood his hesitation. She closed her eyes. "You don't know what you're asking."

"I want you, Robin. I like you a lot."

Robin shook her head. If only he knew how fucked up she was. She had always ruined relationships with good men like Dexter. Her heart was inclined to run from anyone who had the capacity to give her true love. Dexter would never understand that. She would hurt him.

He took a step back then procured his cell phone out of his pants pocket. "I'll call you a cab."

She kept her eyes cast down. "No."

"Yes," he insisted, making the call.

Robin had never felt so rejected. However, she couldn't blame Dexter. He was a good guy. She was a bad girl.

She folded her arms across her chest. "Open the door."

"Five minutes?" he asked the cab driver.

"Unlock the damn door," she said louder.

He still wouldn't do it, so Robin pulled and tugged at the locks.

"Hey," he said gently and gathered her in his arms.

Robin kept shaking her head, wanting to stay exactly where she was standing yet needing to get as far away from him as possible.

"I want you to reach out to me when you're ready for something more serious," he whispered in her ear.

She couldn't respond. However, she let him hold her close until his phone dinged, alerting him the cab was out front. They didn't say goodbye. He unlocked the door and held it open. They stared into each other's eyes one last time.

Robin sighed gravely. "Could you not tell Sonja about this? Please?"

"I won't," he assured her.

She was about to walk out but then paused. "One more thing."

His gorgeous eyes widened.

"Could you not mention Mars either? She doesn't know about us. Neither does Elaine or my sister. Please?"

He frowned as he shook his head slightly. "Whatever."

Robin broke eye contact. "Thanks."

She then stepped out of his house and out of his life.

24 Hours Later

DURING THE FIVE-HOUR FLIGHT FROM JFK TO LAX, Robin couldn't get the conclusion of the previous night out of her mind. She could fall in love with Dexter if she allowed herself to do it. Perhaps she was already in love with him and either didn't know it or refused to acknowledge it.

She currently lived in her Venice Beach studio.

The apartment complex where she'd lived ever since graduating college had been converted to condos, and her old unit had a new resident. After the last three weeks in New York preparing for the art show then giving into her desire for Dexter, it would've been nice to hang around Gran for a few days. Robin hated that Gran had moved to Indian Wells, California, where she spent most of her days golfing and attending events with her new friends, who were also enjoying their golden years. After decades spent taking care of her daughters' daughters, Gran was finally focusing solely on her own happiness. The thought made Robin smile. There was no way she was going to crash Gran's life. Instead, she needed to remember who she desired before her defenses were broken by the sight of Dexter.

She wasn't that far away from her studio when she made a sharp right and headed up Washington Boulevard and back toward the 405. The traffic was stop and go all the way to Sunset Boulevard and even more horrendous as she drove through Westwood to Beverly Hills. However, unlike most people, Robin didn't mind the slowdown. Two months ago, she'd purchased her first convertible roadster. After leaving the hot humidity of NYC, the dryer California heat felt just right on her skin. The smog wasn't chokingly thick either. And more importantly, she was home.

She took a left off the main boulevard and drove up the mountain road until she reached the top, where a lot of celebrities lived. Robin pulled up to Mars's gate and buzzed the house.

"Hello," Lourdes answered.

"Hi, Lourdes, it's Robin. Is Mars in?"

The house manager went deadly silent.

"Hello?" Robin said.

The gate buzzed then slid open.

Robin didn't get a chance to say thank you like she wanted. She parked at the rear of the large house, next to a gray Porsche. Robin had never seen the car before, but Mars changed his cars like most people changed their socks. After turning off her engine, Robin hinged her neck forward to get a good look at Lourdes, who had walked out of the back door, leaving it open. After taking a few steps, Lourdes stopped and stared at her.

Robin sat up straight. The house manager was sending her a message. Lourdes moved down the walkway between the perfectly manicured hedges, carrying a basket of clothes, until she entered the guesthouse.

Once Lourdes was out of sight, Robin exited her vehicle. She walked quickly between the hedges and entered through the open door. She checked the time on her watch as she trekked up the long hallway then up a flight of stairs to the main level. The house had eight bedrooms, but the west wing was where Mars spent most of his time because of its views of the coast. It was after two p.m. Being a working actor, he slept at odd hours. If he was awake, he would be in his office, on the phone with his agent or publicist, both of whom called nonstop. Robin checked his office, but it was empty.

After turning away from that space, she stopped and sighed deeply. Why continue deluding herself? Robin talked herself out of checking his gym and the indoor pool. She decided to cut to the chase and head to his favorite bedroom, the one he always took her to because it had all of his condoms and special sex toys he liked to use to stimulate the pussy. Mars was one of those guys who derived power from watching while he made a woman climax. Actually, his dick was only half hard before that happened. As soon as she cried out in orgasm, he became as hard as steel, and only then could he pound her brains out.

She didn't have to make it to the bedroom to

hear them. A woman was moaning as though she were having the time of her life.

"I'm fucking you hard," Mars shouted.

A strange feeling overcame Robin. She wanted to turn around and head back to her car. There was no need to see or hear more, but the woman's voice sounded familiar.

"Holy fuck me!" she cried.

He grunted like a wild animal. The headboard knocked against the wall. Mars had never fucked her so demonstratively, and fortunately so. She didn't know if it would've turned her on.

Robin's feet weren't ready to proceed yet. She heard a shift in position, then the woman started moaning as if what was happening to her was the most pleasurable thing ever. It was as if Robin's body began moving forward without her permission. When she made it to the doorway, she saw Mars's face between a pair of skinny legs. The woman's eyes were closed. Robin recognized her. Mars and his lover were so consumed by their sex session that neither noticed her.

Slowly, silently, Robin backed away from the room. Her heart and mind were distressed as her feet walked her back to her car.

CHAPTER 4

*R*obin lay curled up in bed with the covers over her head. The fetal position was how she'd spent most of her days and nights. The blackout shades over the windows did a great job of keeping the light at bay. She hated the fact that she could hear the ocean nonstop. Why did people love living on the beach? Robin had decided to pack her bags and move somewhere else as soon as she was able to. A few days after she'd caught Mars and Plume Ashbury fucking, all the gossip rags made the most hurtful announcement ever. Plume and Mars had gotten engaged. On top of that, Plume was pregnant with his first child.

It was still a mystery to her why the public announcements hurt her so much. She recognized the pain her heart was feeling, and in a sick way, she'd been waiting for it to happen. At a certain point in her grieving process, she'd realized she was pained the most by the fact that she was so fucked up and had no idea how to help herself.

The moment Robin decided to fall away from the world, she set her cell phone to only accept calls from her family. She couldn't hide from them. She only had to convince her sister and cousins that all was well in her world whenever they called. She hadn't wanted to hear from anyone else. So far, no one suspected her life had been at a standstill for the past four weeks.

Robin yawned, trapped between the state of wanting to go back to sleep but being wide-awake. So she started remembering Mars with his head between Plume's thin thighs. The way that visual made her feel confused the hell out of her. She wasn't in love with Mars. Half the time, she didn't even like him. She couldn't trust him or rely on him. He was her comfortable uncomfortable. All the men she'd ever been with had been a result of her issues. And she couldn't do it anymore. She couldn't involve herself with another dud.

Her cell phone rang for the first time in six... maybe seven or eight days. She checked the screen and, after taking a deep breath, tapped the answer button.

"Hi, Son," Robin said in the most cheerful voice she could muster. She even faked a smile to make sure she sounded convincing enough.

"Open the door," Sonja demanded.

She scrambled to sit up. "What?"

"Open the damn door, Robin. I'm on your step."

Robin ended the call and sat on the edge of her bed. *Did that really just happen?* She checked her recent calls. It had.

"Shit," she muttered and examined the chaos around her. Dirty plates and cups were on the floor, nightstands, dresser, and the empty side of her bed. She smelled like a sewer. Robin turned to look at herself in the mirror above her dresser. Her hair was wild and greasy, and her face was pale and blotchy. Goodness, she looked like a meth addict.

Now Sonja was ringing the bell over and over. Then her phone rang again.

She tapped answer. "I'm coming."

Sonja hung up before she could.

Robin had to take the industrial elevator down to the ground floor. She owned all three levels of the space that used to be a warehouse. When she opened the metal door, the daylight stabbed her in the eyes, and she had to back into the shade like a vampire.

Sonja gasped and slapped a hand over her heart. "Oh my God, Robbie. What the hell?"

Robin squeezed the top of her head in frustration. "What do you want, Sonja?"

"Are you fucking kidding me? I want to know what the hell is going on with you."

It had been a long time since Robin had tried to look someone in the eyes. Her eyelids were too heavy to do it. "What are you doing here? You're supposed to be in Vancouver."

"You're slurring your words."

"Am I?"

"Okay, come on," Sonja said, zipping past her.

"What?" Robin asked with her eyes half open.

"You're coming with me."

She shook her head. "No."

"Yes," Sonja insisted.

"Well, I don't have my purse or keys, so…"

Sonja pointed at the black leather sofa in Robin's small den area. "I'll go upstairs, pack your bag, get your purse and keys, and then, Robbie, you're coming with me. Capisce?"

Robin didn't have the strength to challenge

Sonja. It was hard to win when her cousin considered the moment a national crisis and was hell-bent on doing something about it. So she went along with Sonja's plan.

ROBIN HEARD SONJA FAINTLY CALLING HER NAME. Her mind wasn't in tune with her body yet, so she had to figure out how she'd arrived at that moment. There'd been a car ride. She had wept the whole way to the Hancock Park estate, the home that Gran had sold to Sonja and Jay before moving to the desert. Robin recalled whimpering as she'd sat in the passenger's seat. Sonja hadn't asked her to explain herself, and Robin was grateful for it. When they'd arrived at the place they considered their primary childhood home, Sonja told her that her old room was ready for her. Robin recalled walking into the space, which had been renovated. Some of her artwork was on the wall. Instead of a full-sized bed, Sonja and Jay had put a king-sized one in the room. Two black leather armchairs faced the bulging window that looked over the garden. The fact that the room was designed to her taste had made Robin cry even more as she'd situated herself under the covers. When she'd fallen asleep again, Robin felt that even though her heart ached, Sonja and Jay had made her know she was deserving of love, so she'd rested more comfortably than she had since finding out Plume and Mars were engaged.

Finally, Robin opened her eyes. The light of a day that would soon fade into evening flowed through the window. The rays, though soft, momentarily stung her eyes.

"Hey, Sonja," Robin whispered as she struggled to sit against the headboard. There were a lot of aches and pangs in her body, but her head felt as if someone were pounding on it.

Sonja sat on the foot of the bed with her arms crossed timidly. "How are you feeling?"

Robin yawned. "Better."

They watched each other carefully.

Sonja cleared her throat. "So Claudia told me you hadn't been taking her calls or answering the door when she came by."

Robin frowned. "She came by?"

Sonja held up five fingers. "Five times."

"Oh."

"Then Dexter told me you were seeing Mars MacAvoy, and everybody knows he's engaged to Plume." Sonja rolled her eyes. She was not a fan of

Plume Ashbury, on or off the screen. "So how long have you been involved with him?"

Robin closed her eyes and sighed gravely. "Too long." She shook her head as tears rushed to her eyes. "And it's not like I didn't expect him to betray me somehow. I don't even know why it hurts so much. This is how all my relationships end. I'm just so tired of it, but I don't know how to stop the cycle." She wiped the tears rolling down her cheeks.

"Oh, sweetie." Sonja hugged her. "You have insight about everyone else's life but your own."

"I know. It's the easiest way to hide my shitty issues."

Sonja leaned back to look at her face. "So what are you going to do about it, Robbie?"

"I don't know what to do about it. I don't know how to be different."

"You always have the answers. I promise you do. Look, if I were you, what would you say to me?"

Robin stared intensely at Sonja's face. The question felt overwhelming. She squeezed her eyes twice. Nope, it didn't help. The headache was still present. "I don't know."

Sonja took her by the hands and held them tight. "Try."

"Okay," Robin said with a tired sigh. "I would tell you Mars MacAvoy is no one to cry over."

"What else?"

"Um…" She twisted her mouth to think. "Why did you get into a relationship you had to keep secret?"

"What do you think that means?"

Robin widened her eyes as thoughts poured through her mind. Sonja's rapid-fire questioning was helping. "I agreed to it because…"

"Because?"

"It was what I was comfortable with."

"Why?"

"I'm scared to be loved for real."

Finally, Sonja smiled tenderly. "So was I. And you know why that is. Are you really going to let your shitty mother and my shitty aunt, Lily Rose, ruin your happiness? I mean, where the fuck is she anyway? I know where she is." Sonja was talking demonstratively with her hands. "She's somewhere in this great big, wide world, worrying and caring about no one but her own self. She's selfish. We're nothing like our mothers, Robin. But you'll never know it unless you put the real you to the test. You see, Gran taught us to be ourselves—the person God made us. I promise that's who you are."

The tears and snot were draining too fast for Robin to keep up with, so Sonja popped up off the bed to grab a box of tissue. When she returned, Robin had an epiphany.

"Here," Sonja said, handing her a tissue.

Robin blew her nose then took two more to wipe her face.

Sonja grabbed the wastebasket, which was against the wall, and held it toward Robin, who disposed of the tissues.

"There," Sonja said.

It had been a long time since Robin smiled, but she did it. "You know what I realized while you were gone?"

"I'm all ears."

"I can spend the rest of my life punishing myself for being Lily Rose's daughter, and she'll never be around to see me self-destruct because she doesn't give a damn if I do or don't."

Sonja pinched her chin delicately. "So get back out there, kiddo, and keep making your life great. Fall in love for real and live happily ever after."

She was about to say that happily ever after didn't exist, but then she remembered Elaine and Zach Lord were genuinely happy, and so were

Sonja and Jay. Robin and her sister, Theresa, were the only ones who were closed off to love.

Robin hung her head. "I don't even know if I want to be an artist anymore."

Sonja took her by the hands again. "Well, figure it out, Robbie. You have the rest of your life to do it."

They hugged each other tight.

"By the way," Robin said as they let go of each other. "How's Dexter doing these days? Is he dating anyone?"

Sonja's eyes widened. "Oh my God, I forgot to tell you. He's dating Claudia."

Robin's heart sank. She couldn't blame anyone but herself for blowing an opportunity to have a stable relationship with Dexter. Plus, she didn't know if she was ready for what he had to offer, at least not yet. It would take time before she learned how to choose the right guy and not end up running away from him a week later. So she put on a fake smile. "Good for him. I mean them." She expanded her manufactured smile. "I'll call her in the morning."

Sonja told her that she had been asleep for nearly sixteen hours. Since Sonja was flying back to Vancouver the next morning, they went over to Elaine and Zach's for dinner. After eating, Zach made a bonfire on the beach and played the harmonica as they sat around the flames. The guy was definitely a billionaire of many talents. A few neighbors joined them as he played popular songs from the nineties, and they drank wine while singing along or mumbling their way through if they couldn't remember the words. Robin hadn't laughed so much in years. The freedom. The family. New friends. A new outlook on life. Finally, she felt happy. At least she did in that moment.

The next morning, slightly hungover but still feeling the good vibes of the previous night's fun while sleeping in Elaine's guest room, Robin called Claudia.

"You make this harder than it should be, Robin," Claudia groused.

"I know," Robin said, determined to sit there and take the tongue-lashing she deserved.

"I urged you to leave him alone. He wasn't good

for you, and he's no good for Plume Ashbury either. Believe me, darling, he's crumbs, and you are too good for him."

"Did he ever proposition you?" Robin asked.

"All the fucking time, but I wouldn't let him touch me with a ten-foot pole. I hope you used condoms with him. Tell me you did."

"All the time."

"Never once did you not use one?"

"Never."

Claudia sighed with relief. "I was so worried about that."

Robin smiled slightly, appreciating the support and concern. Dexter's face came to mind, and she so badly wanted to ask Claudia about her relationship with him, but she decided against it.

"So what next?" Robin asked.

"Next is you finally letting me be your manager. Can you do that? If you can't, then…" She sighed briskly. "You're a great artist, one of the best today, but if you don't want this, then I can't force you any longer. You fight me all the time. I need you to do what I ask you to do. I always ask, you know, but you should say yes."

Robin rubbed her eyes as the cold, hard truth

came to mind. "I don't know if I want it anymore, Claudia."

Claudia became so quiet that Robin thought she'd hung up.

"Claudia?"

"I'm here," she said sharply. "You better figure it out, Robin, because I'm tired of wasting my time. You're supposed to be in Berlin next week. And you were supposed to have the second part of Soulscape finished by now. Have you been working on it?"

She was still rubbing her eyes. "No."

"Are you going to?"

Robin sighed wearily. "Yes, I will."

"I can get you a month's extension for Berlin, but you better come through. Or you tell me right now, do you want me to cancel?"

Yes. "No."

"Okay." Claudia sounded relieved. "But don't embarrass me like this again. When you didn't show up at the studio in Berlin, I had to make excuses for you. I had to let go of your team of helpers, even after they signed the NDAs." She sighed wearily. "I have a reputation for representing the best and most professional artists. Don't screw that up for me."

Robin ate more humble pie and once again apologized to Claudia for not coming through with the second part of the installation project. Actually, she had forgotten all about it, which further made her believe she was ready to walk away from art altogether. But not yet. She would give it one more try to see if she still had the passion to create art in her heart.

CHAPTER 5

THREE MONTHS LATER

*R*obin flopped down in a chair, holding the two cappuccinos she'd just ordered. Her eyes roamed the room, and she cringed. She didn't know why in the world Claudia had picked such a place to meet two hours before she was to appear live on an afternoon talk show to make excuses for her latest disaster. There were hipsters everywhere. Robin didn't really care for snooty mini-adults much, even though many of them were fans of her work. Regardless, she took a sip of coffee and decided not to let the atmosphere bother her.

Robin was back in Brooklyn. That morning, she had taken a cab from Upper Manhattan, across the city, and over the Brooklyn Bridge. At times, she'd had to hold on to her hat as the driver sped up and down avenues, avoiding men at work, road closures, and traffic. The feelings Manhattan gave her as opposed to Brooklyn were remarkably different. Once in Brooklyn, she'd been able to let go of the door handle and breathe. They had soared through a familiar neighborhood, the one where the after-party of her successful exhibit had been held. She would spot a corner, a tree, or a storefront awning under which she and Dexter had made out ferociously.

Robin pinched her lower lip as her mind vividly recalled each kiss, grope, suck, or bite on her neck. She squeezed her eyes tightly shut twice, purging Dexter out of her thoughts, then took *The Berlin Scene*'s art section out of her purse and flipped the pages until she landed on the review of Soulscape Part Two. There were two lines that she couldn't stop reading over and over again.

Soulscape Part Two, the light installation project by Robin Hester, is nothing more than a jumbled mess of Christmas lights and wire. She made an embarrassing showing in Berlin, greatly disappointing fans as many are considering the success of Soulscape Part One a one-hit wonder.

Robin recalled the days and nights she'd spent

in her studio in Berlin, struggling to come up with ideas. She had no vision, but more importantly no desire to be successful. Every morning for two hours, she would sit at a café on the ground floor of her building and watch the buses and locals race by. Everyone looked so stressed, so serious, so pallid. Each morning, she searched her mind for the answer to one question. Was the human race destined to spend the majority of their lives living in misery rather than bliss? Soon her dark mood had begun to flood her. Once it had completely engulfed her, there was no going back.

The good thing was she hadn't shown up the night of the gallery show. She'd known it was a failure when local art students were helping her set up for the exhibition. Heck, they'd known it too. No one had said anything to her about it, though, although she'd seen the dread in their eyes.

The first review she'd read was from the publication in her hand. She was about to read the critical review for what probably was the thousandth time when the magazine was snatched out of her hands.

The smell of perfume pretty much announced Claudia's arrival before Robin could look up.

"I told you to stop reading this," Claudia said as she sat in the chair across from Robin.

"I actually I know it by heart. 'The fact that she had to go all the way to Berlin and bomb is an indication that Hester should rid herself of the fantasy that she's an installation artist and continue to embrace the brush and her oil paints.'"

Claudia rolled her eyes. "This is just one setback. That's all. Next time, you'll do something brilliant, and they'll forget about this."

Robin made her expression blank on purpose. What to do next was still up in the air. The time had come to accept the truth. The reason she'd started making installations was because she had lost her mojo with the brush. Whenever she faced a blank canvas, she had no idea what to paint. Recently, she'd been scribbling messy abstracts that no one would appreciate, certainly not her. Robin was thinking about going back to school and studying something, although she hadn't figured out what yet.

"So are you ready for your interview?" Claudia looked excited.

Robin groaned as she shrugged.

"Really?"

"What?"

"I need you to be different than what you are now during the interview. Tease them with your next installation project, which you will be starting immediately." Claudia combed through her long and shiny raven tresses before taking a drink of her cappuccino. She closed her eyes, seeming to relish the taste.

Robin couldn't help but wonder if that was the expression she held when Dexter brought her sexual pleasure. Suddenly, she was battling jealousy.

"Like it?" Robin asked as soon as Claudia was looking at her again.

"They make the best cappuccino. Reminds me of home."

Robin raised her eyebrows. "And where's home?"

"I never told you?"

"I never asked."

Claudia grunted thoughtfully. "No, you haven't. I was born in Lyon, France."

"Is that where you grew up?"

"I grew up in Portland."

"Oregon?"

"Yes," she said sharply, tugging at her scarf. Her pretty face was red. She was clearly agitated.

Robin figured Claudia was merely another

Z. L. ARKADIE

person who had made herself into what she believed would be the version people would respond to, hence the fake accent. However, since they were getting personal, Robin figured it was time to ask one more question, the one she'd been dying to ask for a long time. "So how's it going with Dexter?"

"Dexter Frampton?" Claudia asked with a high-pitched voice.

"Aren't the two of you dating?" Robin asked.

Claudia slightly turned her head. "How long have you held that question?"

Robin shrugged. "For a while."

"Have you been thinking this whole time I've been screwing the man you're in love with?"

She slapped herself on the chest. "In love?" *Am I in love with Dexter?* Love was such a serious word to throw around so haphazardly.

Claudia watched her with one eye narrowed. "Nothing ever happened between him and I, but it's not because I didn't want it to. If he would have wanted me, I would've said something to you. Remember the night I mentioned that I saw you leaving the after-party with Dexter?"

Robin readjusted in her seat. "Yes, I do."

"Remember what you said?"

She closed her eyes and nodded. "I said it was

78

nothing and that I was heading back to LA to finally tell Mars that I loved him."

"Then I asked if Dexter was fair game, and you said?"

Robin tried to remember Claudia asking her that. She was sure Claudia had, but there'd been so much on her mind that night that she had probably ignored half the things that had come out of Claudia's mouth.

"You said, 'Of course.'"

Her mouth fell open. "I did?"

"Yes. You did. I pursued him. But he wasn't interested."

Robin was overwhelmed by the sense of relief. "Then you never dated?"

"I traveled to Vancouver, pretending as though I had business there." She rolled her eyes. "I know—I was shameless. I said I was in town and asked if he would like to have dinner. He said yes. Sonja and the rest of the cast and crew were at the same restaurant. She must've seen me try every move in my book on him." She raised a finger. "I mean no man can resist me." She grinned at a man across the room, and he smiled shyly, turning red. Then she turned to her left and gave another guy a smoldering look. He waved at her. Then Claudia turned back to Robin and shrugged. "See? So I did not expect Dexter Frampton to resist me. But he was never into me. He's into you."

Robin felt her eyes grow wide. Claudia sounded so sure about how Dexter felt about her, but he hadn't even tried to contact her since the last time they'd kissed.

Claudia's red lips cracked in a lopsided grin. "But when he gets over you, I'll be there to soothe him."

Robin frowned. "Really?" *Did Claudia just really say that?*

"For sure. He's a catch, and he's not going to pine after you forever. But anyway"—Claudia flopped a hand dismissively—"we have to focus on what's ahead of us. Are you ready for your interview with Krista? Do we have to do some media coaching first?"

It took a moment for Robin to recuperate from what she had just learned. For so long, she'd let herself believe Dexter and Claudia were sexually involved. Of course she could've asked Sonja for an update, but the truth was Robin hadn't wanted to know his exact relationship status. She still needed time to figure out if she could believe in herself when it came to matters of the heart.

"Um, no. Don't need to prepare," Robin finally said.

Claudia hopped to her feet. "Then okay. Let's go."

Robin stood slowly, thinking that perhaps she should pay Dexter a visit after the interview. *Maybe not.*

THE STUDIO WAS IN MANHATTAN, AND ON THE drive over, Claudia engaged Robin in media prep anyway and threw a barrage of questions at her. When Robin didn't answer the way Claudia would like, her manager wrote down the correct response and made Robin read it until she remembered it. As soon as their car pulled up in front of the studio, an eager-looking production assistant wearing head-phones was waiting for them.

"Good morning, Miss Hester," the PA said in a dry tone.

Robin smiled tightly. "Good morning." Her nerves were through the roof.

"Follow me, please." The PA walked off fast, but Robin remained stationary after noticing Claudia didn't get out of the vehicle.

"I have a meeting with another client, but"—she held up her iPhone and wiggled it—"I have access to the live feed, so I'll be watching."

Robin took the fact that Claudia wouldn't be in the building as a sign that the announcement she planned to make was the right decision.

"Okay, then," Robin said, waving goodbye.

Claudia aimed her finger at Robin with a look of warning in her eyes. "Don't screw this up."

Robin turned her back on the car.

"I mean it," Claudia said.

Robin raised a hand to put her manager at ease, even though she planned on torpedoing her career. She smiled tightly at the PA again.

"I'm Tammy," the PA said, seamlessly picking up where she'd left off.

Robin followed Tammy into the studio.

THINGS WENT FAST FROM THAT POINT ON. THE production people insisted she sit in the makeup chair, even though Robin tried to convince them she looked better without the face paint. However, they split the difference and made her look natural. Apparently, the black turtleneck and black pants she was wearing weren't complimentary to the camera either. They made her change into a light-blue turtleneck but allowed her to keep on the black pants since she wouldn't be walking live on set.

Once Robin's hair and makeup were done and she was mic'd up, Tammy escorted her to the green-room, where there were muffins, bagels, warm breakfast burritos, hot biscuits with cheese, water, coffee, tea, and of course, wine. Robin knew to beware of the wine trap. It was there to get the guests loose so that they would give more revealing interviews. So instead of grabbing a glass of truth serum to calm her nerves, she slathered a lot of maple syrup cream cheese on a blueberry muffin. She took her second bite, chewing slowly, savoring every moment of deliciousness. She should go on an eating spree around Europe once she was free from the art world. She would eat as much pasta, cheese, and pastries as she wanted. In the last three months, she had lost another fifteen pounds on top of her already slight frame because she had been so stressed. If Gran could see her so thin, she would've declared Robin's condition dire and made sure she consumed three square meals a day and two snacks just to get back to a healthy weight.

Robin suddenly remembered the invitation

she'd received to attend Jacques Blanchard's birthday party in Bordeaux, France. The party was scheduled for the end of December, which was next month. Maybe she would fly to France early and go to Paris to visit with friends she had neglected over the years. As soon as her interview was over, she would book a flight and do just that. "That's it," Robin said to herself with her eyes closed as she savored her third bite of the muffin.

"What's it?" asked a voice that sounded familiar.

Her eyes popped open. She blinked twice, thinking that her eyes were deceiving her. "Dexter?"

"Good morning, Robin. Or should I say good afternoon?" He sounded so formal. Not only that, but his beautiful eyes were cold. Claudia was wrong. He certainly had no love for her.

CHAPTER 6

*D*exter's presence filled the doorway. He wore a pair of black slacks that fit his athletic thighs perfectly. And his light-blue sweater matched his eyes.

"What are you doing here?" she asked.

"I'm on the show today."

Her mouth fell open as he slid his cell phone out of his pocket and started interacting with the screen.

"Did you know I would be here?"

He snorted cynically.

She waited for him to say something else, but apparently, the snort was all she was going to get. And she hated the snort. It sounded dismissive and belittling. He was behaving like a dick.

"So how have you been?" he asked, even though he still wasn't looking at her.

Robin gathered her lips. She wanted to pout but decided there should be at least one adult in the room. "I'm okay."

Finally, he looked up. "Just okay?"

She nodded stiffly. For some reason, him asking her that made her want to cry. But she fought the urge to do it.

A concerned expression came over his face as he flipped the silent button on his phone and stuffed it back in his pocket. "Listen…"

The door opened. Tammy announced it was time for them to join Krista and Todd, the hosts. Dexter took Tammy's place holding the door open. As Robin passed him, that giddy energy fluttered through her, which confirmed that something special flooded through her whenever she was in Dexter Frampton's presence.

They were on the move again. But it felt like the night they'd walked down the hallway in Elaine's old house. Dexter's presence embraced her from behind. Robin was still processing the fact that he would be joining her during the interview. There was no way Claudia knew. Robin was positive her manager would've told her.

They made it to the set. The female announcer said Robin's name, and an audience, mostly composed of hipsters, stood and applauded. Then she announced that the day's mystery guest was also present. Apparently, that was Dexter.

Krista shook Robin's hand. "Welcome!" She flapped her eyelashes when she greeted Dexter.

Goodness, does every woman in the world flirt with him?

"Glad you could make it," Todd said and shook both their hands.

They were asked to take their seats. Krista made sure Dexter sat next to her. Robin pressed her lips together, hiding how crazy that drove her.

"Dexter, I'm so happy you could make it last minute," Krista said.

He glanced at Robin. "No problem."

Robin caught Krista watching her in a very curious manner, which made her turn to Dexter. "Did you know I was scheduled to be on the show today?" she whispered.

He winked at her. "Not everything's about you."

"I asked a direct question. Do you have a direct answer?"

Dexter smirked. "Yes, I have a direct answer."

"Is yes your answer?"

"No, yes is not my answer."

"Getting ready to go live," the floor director announced.

Robin ripped her frown off of Dexter and sat up straight. Everyone within earshot was watching them. Her emotions were surging too high for her to be embarrassed. Dexter always had the ability to get her going in a negative or positive way. *Why is that?*

Robin folded her arms and shook her head. If only she could walk off the set. Being there and making her announcement on that show no longer felt like the right decision. Perhaps she wouldn't do it.

"In five, four, three, two, one." The floor manager counted down then cued the hosts.

"We're back with two people who are making waves throughout the city for two very different reasons," Krista said. "Robin Hester."

The crowd applauded.

"And Dexter Frampton."

The audience clapped again.

The only waves Robin was making at the moment were bombing at her last showing in Berlin. She wondered if that was what Krista meant.

"Great, Krista," Todd said. "So let's get to it.

Robin, your light installation, Soulscape Part One, people are still talking about it, and everyone still wants to know what was the inspiration behind it?"

Robin drew a blank. Inspiration felt like a lost existence. "Um, light…" She balled her hands into fists, trying to think harder. "Light is"—she shook her head—"all around us."

"Right, right…" Todd said. "But people were literally walking out of your exhibit crying."

"Or kissing," Krista said excitedly. "I've even seen people kissing."

"Then you showed in Berlin," Todd said.

Finally, what Robin knew was coming had arrived. She threw up a hand. "Stop."

The hosts watched her in surprise.

"I didn't do so well in Berlin."

"Why do you think that is?" Dexter asked.

She turned to look at him. Once again, his eyes captured her special attention. *Could they have been my inspiration for Soulscape Part One?* The first night she'd fantasized about being with Dexter was after dinner at Elaine's over a year ago. No matter how much of his appearance she would forget, she remembered his eyes with flawless accuracy. Then she had an epiphany.

"Um…" She was no longer able to deny the truth. "I lost my inspiration."

"The inspiration that you can't remember?" Dexter asked.

Her mouth fell open. Yes, she could remember what had inspired her, but there was no way she was going to say it on live TV.

"You two seem to have a very interesting relationship," Krista said, clearly attempting to regain control of the discussion.

"I can remember it," Robin said, still staring into Dexter's eyes.

"Remember what?" Todd asked, wearing his painted-on smile.

"About what inspires me."

"Then by all means, let us know what it is," Dexter said.

Robin faced Krista again. "My inspiration is that I'm all out of it. That's why I'm here today. I'm hanging up my art for a while. Probably forever."

The audience rumbled, then one boo led to another and another until the jeers filled the entire studio.

Robin felt as if she were having an out-of-body experience.

Finally, the floor manager got everyone to settle

down. However, she tried not to look directly at her pissed fans.

"Does it have anything to do with part two of Soulscape not being received well?" Krista asked.

The audience booed again. Apparently, they didn't believe what the critics had written. That was some consolation.

Dexter raised a hand to quiet them. When the noise simmered, he said, "I think your giving up is a cop-out."

"Don't worry, Dexter, we'll get to you soon," Todd said through that same irritating fake smile, which suddenly looked like the expression one sees before an unexpected boom is lowered.

"No way." Dexter had so much intensity in his body and voice. "You mentioned we know each other. Yeah, I know Robin Hester. I know she can't commit to anything that's good for her."

"Ha. That's not true," Robin said, even though she knew it was.

Dexter's eyes glinted. "When shit gets hard, you start running."

"Sorry for the beep," Krista said to the audience, smiling.

Dexter opened his arms to the audience. "You

have a lot of fans in the room. Why don't you prove to them they weren't admiring a phony?"

Robin's mouth fell open as her gaze bounced from Krista to Todd then to the audience. "Phony?"

"Show them that you're dedicated to them. Right, Krista? Right, Todd?"

Krista and Todd looked at each other as though they knew they'd better go along with the wrong turn their segment was taking. They'd lost complete control to Dexter.

"Okay, okay, quiet down," Todd said, gesturing to the audience to bring down the noise.

Krista smiled at the table. "Right, right…"

"Show us, show us, show us," the audience repeated.

"All right," Todd sang, the white teeth of his practiced smile gleaming. "We're going on break, and we'll be right back."

The hosts held their smiles until the floor manager gave them the all clear.

Krista jumped out of her seat and leaned over Dexter. "What the fuck is wrong with you, Dexter Frampton?" The cue cards that were in front of her flew everywhere.

Being the gentleman that he was at heart, Dexter bent over to pick up the falling cue cards.

"You should be happy. This was the most exciting this show's been since it aired."

"That's not true—that's just not true," Todd said, shaking a finger.

"What's this?" Dexter asked, holding up one of the cards to Krista.

"So Robin Hester, what about it?" an audience member asked.

Robin's attention bopped from Dexter to the hipster and back to Dexter.

"Are you really fucking quitting?" another hipster asked. "Because that's what quitters do."

"Or maybe you *are* a phony," the first guy said.

"I'm not a phony," she barely said, halfway believing she was. Never had she felt so inadequate.

She was wondering what to do next as she watched Krista snatch the cue card out of Dexter's hand. They were staring at each other like the calm before the storm.

"We're coming back in sixty seconds," the floor manager announced.

"Good try." Dexter winked at Krista and shot to his feet then started pulling at his shirt to take off his microphone.

So much was happening at once that Robin was dizzy trying to figure out who to focus on.

"Is it true?" Krista asked Dexter.

Dexter just shook his head.

"We have proof," Todd said.

"Another break?" the floor manager asked whomever was in her ear.

The audience was leaving in droves, casting their Robin Hester signs on the ground.

"Okay," Robin shouted at them.

Most of her fans stopped to look at her.

"I'll try again. Okay?"

Dexter put a hand on Robin's shoulder. "Good for you." His tone was rigid but sincere.

Her mouth fell open as she watched him walk confidently across the studio and leave.

"Yes, okay… Yes." The floor manager walked toward Robin. "Um, Miss Hester?"

"What?" Robin asked sharply.

"If you don't mind following me out of the studio, please. Your segment is over."

ROBIN LAY ON TOP OF THE BED IN HER HOTEL ROOM and stared at the ceiling. It was as if she were frozen in place. What the hell had happened at WBLAT? The afternoon had felt truly surreal.

Apparently, they'd asked her to leave after Dexter had stormed off to save face. However, as Robin had walked out of the studio, Krista had yelled that Robin would never get press from her or anyone else she knew. Krista's final words had been "And congratulations on failing! You're lucky I didn't get to my question about Mars MacAvoy. I know you were fucking him and Dexter Frampton too!"

Krista's accusation had made her feel cheap. First of all, she'd never had sex with Dexter, even though she wanted to. Secondly, what she and Mars had had was more than mere sex to her, even though it had turned out to be only sex. Robin smashed her palms over her eyes and groaned. If only today had never happened.

Suddenly, her cell phone rang, and she sat straight up. Maybe it was Dexter. She hoped so as she reached over and swiped her device off the nightstand.

"Hello," she said.

"What the hell happened on that talk show today?"

"Terry?" It was her sister, Theresa.

"Yeah, you looked like a fool. And really, how the hell are you twenty-eight years old and retiring already? Does Gran know about this scheme of yours?"

If only she had checked the name on the screen before answering, she could've been better prepared to engage with her sister's strong personality. All she needed were a few more seconds to turn on her apathy switch so she wouldn't take Theresa's briskness so personal.

Robin squeezed her eyes shut, trying to ease the headache that had just crept up on her. "First of all, I'm thirty now. And how did you even see the interview? They're a local channel in New York."

"There's internet TV. You do know that, right?"

She took a steadying breath. "Terry, could you not today? Because I really, really don't feel—"

"No. I have to, Robbie. I mean, you're in fucking crisis right now!"

Robin pulled the phone back because Terry was yelling in her ear. However, she did hear her say, "I'm just doing my big sister's job. Are you moping? You better not be moping. Why don't you just come stay with me for a while?"

She brought the phone back to her ear. *That would be a serious negative.* "Um, no."

"Then what's your plan? I need to hear it. Give it to me."

It was as though a tsunami suddenly crashed against her soul. That was the amount of stress Theresa had the power to bring to her life. "I'm going to do Soulscape Part Two all over again."

"The project that failed?"

"Yes, Terry. The one that failed."

"Is that smart?"

She wanted to whine that she didn't know, but the conversation they were having was unhealthy in so many ways.

"Terry?" she finally asked, keeping her voice calm.

"What?" Theresa snapped.

"How are *you*?"

"Me?"

"Yes, you."

"Why are you asking how I am when you're the one in—"

"Because I know you, and you're at your most offensive when you're engaging in transference."

"Transference?"

"Yes. You're transferring your issues onto me. So what are you losing control of right now?"

Theresa went dead silent, which further let Robin know she was on the right track.

"Nothing," Theresa barked. "Well… something."

Robin rolled her eyes as she nodded. "Okay, what is it? Give it to me."

"My neighbor."

"What about your neighbor?"

Theresa fell silent again. "Forget about it. Listen, I have to go. Are you going to be okay?"

"Yes. I'll be fine," Robin replied in her most composed voice.

"Then that's that. I love you," she said with a severe lack of emotion, although Robin knew she sincerely meant it.

"I know. I love you too."

They both said goodbye to each other. Robin turned her phone off before dropping it on the bed beside her. There was a knock at the door. She groaned because she knew it was Claudia, the one person she didn't want to see after that call with Theresa.

"Here I come," she called and made herself get up. But when she opened the door, she got the surprise of her life. "What are you doing here?"

Those hypnotizing baby blues that belonged to Dexter Frampton were looking at her. Whenever she stood close to him, her eyes probed him deeply.

With each encounter, she saw a new trait to fixate on. This time, it was his lips. They were the perfect amount of plump. No wonder she loved kissing them. He still smelled just as delicious as he had earlier.

"I called Claudia, and she told me where you were staying."

Robin rolled her eyes and groaned. "Oh, Claudia. I haven't talked to her yet."

"I told her about the promise you made to your fans in the studio this afternoon."

Her eyes expanded. "You did?"

"After that interview, I had to soften her up by telling her something good. But listen…" His smirk was the right kind of naughty. "I'm here because I want to make you an offer you can't refuse."

That was when Robin became cognizant of the fact that they were alone in the doorway of her hotel room with the bed only six feet away. She was slightly panicked by what to do next. Having him so close made her desire a redo of the last time she was with him at his townhouse. This time, the idea of Mars MacAvoy wasn't standing in their way.

"What kind of offer?" she barely asked.

"You were serious about what you said to your fans earlier, weren't you?"

"What did I say?" She had to ask because as usual, prolonged contact with Dexter Frampton made her somewhat scatterbrained.

"You're going to stick around and recreate Soulscape Part Two."

She cleared the frog out of her throat. "Oh, that's right. Yes." Robin was starting to regret putting that out in the universe so people could hold her accountable for it.

"Then why don't you stay with me?"

Robin felt her eyes grow wide. "Seriously?"

She didn't think his smirk could get sexier. "Yeah, seriously," he said.

The cat had her tongue, so to speak. It wasn't a matter of whether she wanted to take him up on his offer—because she wanted to. But she feared that if she said yes, then when it came to Dexter Frampton, she would finally be entering the point of no return.

CHAPTER 7

*R*obin had said yes and was sitting in the back seat of Dexter's chauffeured car. Being driven around in his brand-new Lincoln Continental felt strange. She could've never guessed he was one of those guys who paid for his own personal driver. Regardless, he had put a lot of distance between them, so much so that he nearly clung to the door. Whomever he was texting had his complete attention, which gave Robin a fair amount of discomfort. For some reason, she wanted his full attention. In actuality, they had a lot to talk about, starting with the last time they'd kissed.

Robin kept glancing at him, taking note of how he grinned from ear to ear as his fingers tapped away on the screen.

"New girlfriend?" she blurted, wishing she could take those words back.

He looked at her with a satisfied grin. "It's your cousin. Sonja saw us on TV this morning. She asked if I would tell you to turn on your phone, but I told her no because you're with me now." He winked at her, and she skipped a breath. Dexter tapped out one last response then slid his phone back into his pants pocket.

Now that she had his attention, Robin had no idea what to say. So they remained silent for a while. She knew he was as nervous as she was. Her breaths were unsteady, and her head was spinning.

What next? We should kiss… We should make out like there's no tomorrow…

"What are you thinking?" Dexter asked.

Robin jumped nervously. "Nothing."

He grinned coyly. "Nothing?"

Her brain had to come up with something fast, so she thought about something she'd been curious about since it had happened. "Well, I do have a question."

"I'm all ears."

She angled the front of her body toward him. "What was on that cue card earlier?"

His flirtatious smile faded fast. "You mean at the studio?"

"Yeah." Robin purposely kept her tone light since she could sense his sudden trepidation.

He turned his glare toward the window.

Robin immediately felt as though it were best to forget she had ever asked about the strange exchange between him and Krista. "You don't have to answer."

Dexter was watching her again. Goodness, she loved when he looked at her.

"It's a long story, and I'd rather keep it to myself unless I don't have the privilege of doing that anymore," he said.

She nodded. "That's fair. But I have another question."

He tilted his head as if to say, "Let's hear it."

"A Lincoln Continental with your own personal driver? I didn't picture you as the type to get around the city like this."

He chuckled as though he were thankful for the change in subject. "What type did you picture me as?"

She shrugged. "I thought of you as someone who needed to convince people you were the good old average Joe."

He frowned then grunted thoughtfully. "What made you think that?"

"Am I wrong?"

"No."

She raised her eyebrows, surprised that he'd not only answered quickly but honestly.

"However, I'm a busy person. I have meetings all over the city all day long. I have to get to the airport without delay. I have two daughters who attend events and are involved in extracurricular activities. I like to make sure they get from point A to point B safely, and other than Luddie and I"—he reached out and squeezed his driver's shoulder—"Vick here is the only other person I trust to do that."

Vick glanced at her in the rearview mirror. His eyes were smiling. It was nice to discover something else about Dexter that made him a rare specimen. He was an attentive father.

His gaze consumed her. "You're very beautiful, Robin."

Heat raced through her palms. Compliments regarding her looks were common, but it was the first time she'd actually felt how attractive she truly was. Robin dropped her face bashfully. "Thank you."

"Remember when we were at my house last?"

She kept her eyes on her lap. "I remember."

"I've replayed that night in my head too many times to count. In every instance, I take you to bed and finish you off."

After a few beats of silence, she looked at him. His rousing blue eyes were on fire.

"Can I ask you something?" he finally said.

She couldn't speak, so she nodded.

"What made you pick Mars MacAvoy?"

The floaty feeling in her head slowly began to subside. "What do you mean by pick him?"

"You're sensible, beautiful, and smart as hell. What do you have in common with Mars MacAvoy?"

The truth made her appear shallow and unsteady, so under no circumstances was she going to say it.

"Because you see, my take is your relationship with the guy was physical. Am *I* wrong?"

That was a question she was willing to answer. "No."

He smiled slightly. "You know he was the lead actor on the first film I ever wrote and produced for a studio—*The Raging Dark.* Ever heard of it?"

She shook her head. "I'm not a movie watcher."

"No?" He sounded ultra-surprised.

"No. The last time I watched a movie was in high school. It was Jay's first major film."

"Ah," he said, intrigued. "Your family has known Jay West for a long time."

"Since we were kids." She smiled as she fondly thought of the shaggy-haired blond boy. "I used to have a crush on him. I never told anyone that before, but I did. However, he's always been in love with Sonja." She sighed nostalgically. "Everyone loved Sonja more—Gran, Jay, Elaine, Theresa, me…" A familiar sad feeling gripped her insides, making her feel nauseated.

"More than who?" Dexter asked.

She attached her gaze to his face. "What?"

"You said everyone loved Sonja more—more than who? You?"

Her mouth gaped as they stared at each other. She had already said too much. No one had been privy to her inner pain of always being number two or three or four, yet she had shared it with Dexter. The waiting look on his face was patient and empathetic.

Robin gulped. "Yes," she barely said.

After a moment of time in which she hoped he wanted to kiss her just as much as she wanted to be kissed, he tapped the back of the front passenger's seat. "Vick, roll the window up and keep driving until I knock," Dexter said.

As the glass between the front and back of the luxury vehicle rolled up, Dexter leaned toward her. Her body and lips waited impatiently for contact as the glass stopped halfway up.

"Dexter," Vick said.

Robin released the breath she'd been holding as Dexter ripped his eyes away from her and blinked himself out of a lustful daze. "Yeah, Vick."

"You might want to take a look at this." Vick pointed at a crowd of approximately twenty people gathered in front of Dexter's brownstone. Robin scooted to the edge of her seat to get a better look. A lot of men were carrying cameras.

"Shit," he muttered. "Turn the car around now."

"What's going on? Are your daughters all right?" Robin asked.

"Yes. My daughters are with their mother for the week." Dexter rubbed his face. "I can't go home right now. Shit."

"Why? What's going on?"

"It was Krista. Fucking Krista Roberts," Dexter said under his breath.

"What about Krista?" Robin asked.

The car bolted up the street, going toward the harbor. "Where should I go, Dexter?" Vick asked.

Dexter massaged his temples. "I gotta think."

Robin gathered that whatever had been on the cue card had something to do with the cameras in front of Dexter's brownstone. He seemed equally frazzled and angered by the activity. His dubious expression seemed to see right through Robin. "Mariana and Maribel," he whispered. Then he put a hand on his driver's shoulder. "Vick, pull over. I think we can get ahead of this."

"Ahead of what?" Robin asked.

The car pulled over, and Dexter opened the door. "I'll tell you along the way. Let me get your door." He got out then opened the door for Robin.

Her feet landed on the curb. They were standing face-to-face. Before she could insist that he start explaining, Dexter wrapped his arms around her, and her head was spinning because he was kissing her deeply.

CHAPTER 8

*R*obin followed Claudia as her manager led her down the cement hallway. They were in a warehouse, which had been converted to luxury condos in DUMBO, a small neighborhood in Brooklyn.

After that first kiss, Robin and Dexter made out even more. In between their sessions, they devised a plan to keep him hidden. Dexter still hadn't told her exactly why men with cameras were ready to ravish his privacy but said he would as soon as they were tucked away safely. He did, however, call the headmaster of his daughters' school to make sure they weren't being stalked by nosy reporters. They weren't, although the headmaster reported hearing news about Dexter. When Dexter called his ex-wife, Luddie, he found out she'd heard as well. "Between you and I, yes, it's true," he told her.

Luddie must've had an excitable reaction because he said, "Not here, not now, Luddie. Just keep the girls with you for a while. I'm going to have to lay low."

Luddie said something that made him think. Robin could see it in his expression. But instead of replying to his ex, all he said was thanks and that he would call the girls when he could.

"What's the story that's about you?" Robin asked as soon as he ended the call.

He pinched his eyebrows and sighed forcefully. "Who did you vote for in the last election?"

Robin jerked her head back, wondering what the rumor had to do with the president. "I voted for Stanford Leary."

"He lost."

"I know." She rolled her eyes. "The other guy, who does nothing but lace the pocketbooks of large corporations, got a second term."

"My father is the other guy, the one who won."

Her mouth fell open. "No way. Raymond Harrison?"

Dexter nodded.

"Does he know you're his son?"

"Yes." His tone was assured.

"Are you 'a love child'?" she asked, drawing air quotes.

"Yes," he replied then scowled as if admitting it made him ache. Dexter started dialing another number on his phone.

"Who are you calling?" Robin pulled her surprise together enough to ask.

"I'm calling you a cab. I'm going somewhere and hanging low for a while."

She immediately put her hand on top of his. "No. Stay with me. I'll call Claudia and have her figure out my studio situation ASAP. Usually, I rent work-life space. Why don't you just hang there with me for a while?" Robin could feel her heart beating out of her chest. She was quite surprised that she had asked him to stay with her and totally expected him to turn her down.

"I would like that," Dexter said, much to her surprise. He took the liberty of drawing her close to him, which was something Mars and all of her previous boyfriends had only done when it was time for sex. "I would like that very much," he said breathlessly.

Then her head was spinning because they were kissing again.

When their lips parted and while her head was still loopy, she called Claudia to ask if her manager could find her some studio space.

"I'm way ahead of you. I already found you a place. Meet me there in half an hour," Claudia said.

"A half hour?" Robin didn't know Brooklyn very well so she was looking for confirmation from Dexter on whether or not that timeframe was feasible.

"Two hours," he whispered.

Claudia took a long pause before agreeing to meet her in two hours.

Robin and Dexter walked nearly three miles to get to their destination. They were an hour late from stopping so often to make out feverishly in an alley, on a private corner, or against a tree in a small urban park. By the time Robin arrived in front of the large renovated building along the river, she was hyped up on dopamine and oxytocin.

After Robin apologized for being late, Claudia studied her with a look that could kill. "You're an hour late."

"I know. I'm sorry."

"Did you walk here?"

"I did."

Her eyes became even narrower. "Just come on."

On the way to the penthouse floor, Claudia continued giving Robin the business about not answering her calls and checking out of the hotel room without letting her know.

"I never had a client who didn't answer my calls. It's rude and disrespectful. Have you ever seen a therapist?" Claudia asked as they stopped in front of the unit.

"Many," Robin replied.

"Well…" She stuck a key in the lock. "I can arrange an appointment for you with one of the best in Manhattan."

Robin held up a hand. "I'm good."

"You don't look good to me. You're sweating, and it's cold out. It's not raining, at least not yet." She studied Robin with narrowed eyes as she turned another lock. "Are you an addict? Is that it?"

"An addict?"

"Yes." Claudia stood straight. "A drug addict."

Robin burst out laughing then slapped a hand over her mouth.

Claudia rolled her eyes as she shook her head.

"It's not funny." She pushed open the large metal door.

"No, Claudia. I'm not on drugs."

As Robin walked into the wide-open space, she kept moving toward the view. The block cement, steel, and wires of the Manhattan Bridge accented buildings of all sizes, shapes, and materials looming in the background. Lower Manhattan did nothing to inspire her. Robin pressed a hand over her heart. It was what was in her chest that made her want to remain in the city.

"The sky is always closer to the earth on the East Coast. Have you ever noticed that?" Robin asked.

Claudia glared at her. "Are you impaired?"

Robin ripped her gaze away from the heaviness beyond the floor-to-ceiling windows and set it on her manager. "What?"

"Because we can't be successful together if you're not honest with me about the shit you're putting in your body. Maybe that's why you haven't been focused lately."

"What am I putting in my body?"

Claudia folded her arms stubbornly. "Drugs, perhaps."

Robin rolled her eyes.

"Look at you. You're anxious, like you're coming off a high or something."

"Could you stop saying that I'm high. I told you I wasn't." Then her mind flashed back to her make-out sessions with Dexter on their long walk. He was so horny, biting and sucking her hard nipples through her shirt and rubbing her clit through her skinny jeans. His breath was warm in her ear and on her neck as he whispered to her to say when she felt it. Then she would say it, and he would rub faster and harder until she climaxed.

"Okay, but remember, we can't make this work between us if you're lying to me."

She *was* lying. "I'm not lying to you. Well, just a little."

Claudia threw her hands up demonstratively. "I knew it!" Her accent was strong again.

"I'm not high." Robin smiled as she walked over and put her hands on Claudia's shoulders. "But yes, I did leave my hotel room. I have been walking a lot this afternoon…"

"Where's your luggage?" Claudia asked.

Robin's eyes grew wide. The fact that Claudia was observant enough to ask that question was the reason Robin had continued letting the woman manage her career. Claudia was very astute. Not much got past her.

"The hotel is holding it, and as soon as I call them, they'll send it over."

Claudia's eyes roamed Robin's face. Robin worked extra hard to make herself appear credible.

"Okay." Claudia's unwavering smile made her look happy for the first time since they'd met up in front of the building.

Robin stifled a sigh of relief.

Claudia strolled deeper into the unit. "Well, what do you think about your new home for a while?"

"I love it," Robin said. "I mean, I really do."

Claudia's fingers swept the top of the sofa. "Well, it's three thousand square feet, fifteen hundred downstairs and fifteen upstairs, and that's not including your nine-hundred-square-foot studio on the third floor. That's where you'll work, of course. The unit is fully loaded."

Claudia explained how the apartment had been on the market for over a year, but the owners had just put it up for rent the day before, and a list of people were interested.

"But I told them you were interested in it, and they made it available for you right away. And I had the refrigerator stocked this morning because when you work, you hibernate." She dangled the keys. "Get ready to catch." She tossed them, and Robin caught the keys.

"They said if you ever decide to buy this place, they'll make you a good deal, " Claudia said.

"Then the owners know me?"

"This way." Claudia escorted her upstairs to a full art studio, which had some of Robin's best paintings hanging on the wall. One of them was The Glory of Nothing. She stood in front of it. Goodness, she loved that painting and had hated to sell it, but one of her patrons had been roaming around her studio, going into spaces that were off-limits, and had found it sitting on the easel, basking in the Venice Beach sunset. He'd offered her four hundred thousand dollars for it, which was a proposition she couldn't refuse.

"Dugan Gillespie owns this place?" Robin asked.

Claudia's lips stretched into a satisfied smile. Apparently, she was pretty proud of herself for landing Robin a space owned by such a rich and powerful man. "Yes indeed."

Robin nodded. "You did well, Claudia. Thank you."

Claudia shook her fists in celebration. "Yes! That's what I like to hear. Now it's time for you to redeem your reputation and mine too." As she left, she turned to give Robin a few parting words. "Now get to work."

ot even two minutes after Claudia left, the door buzzed. Robin thought it was Claudia returning because she had forgotten to tell her something, but after looking through the peephole, she saw the beautiful blue-eyed man who'd been filling her lust tank all morning. He'd been waiting at Empire Stores for Robin to finish her business with Claudia.

Robin tugged the door open.

"I was going to head over to *FEED* and get you," she said.

Dexter smirked sexily while holding up two coffees. "Someone who lives here let me in."

Robin raised her eyebrows coyly. "Let me guess, a female?"

He winked then handed her one of the cups. "This one's for you. Take a sip."

She smiled flirtatiously, which was something she rarely did, as she took a taste. "Umm… Medium roast with half-and-half. Did you call Sonja to ask her what's my usual?"

A quick lift of the eyebrows and his syrupy smile made her panties wetter.

"If you let me in, I'll explain," he said.

"Oh." She stepped back to let him pass.

He maintained eye contact as he stepped over the threshold. "Let me have this." He took her coffee and set it on top of a shellacked cabinet. Once his hands and hers were free, he drew her against him and kissed her so deep her toes curled.

Robin let the flavors of his mouth and the softness of his tongue arouse her beyond normal levels. It was still hard to believe she was actually giving herself to the one man she had resisted for so long. She was so wet and ready for him to ravish her, especially since once again, his rock-solid erection felt eager to gain access to her warm, dripping wet pussy.

One moment led to the next. Dexter seemed to force his mouth to abandon hers. Her half-opened eyes watched him as she caught her breaths. He scanned the room, then he took her by the hand and guided her to the sofa.

What should have occurred over a year ago was finally about to happen. The thought made Robin wetter. He pulled off one of her ankle boots then the next. Their hazy gazes remained connected as he unbuttoned, unzipped, and pulled down her pants.

Dexter freed his erection then parted her knees. Robin closed her eyes to wait. Then he did it. Dexter Frampton thrust his erection inside her. He went deep, hard. Her heart felt as if it would explode. The swarm of emotions soaring through her could not be contained.

Dexter's baby blues connecting with her hazel eyes ignited her desire. His breath crashed then melted with hers, arousing her. In, out, in, out. His massive cock filled every nook and cranny of her. Gosh, his lovemaking had so many staccatos and tempos as he sucked her bottom lip then her top one before diving deep into her mouth with his eager tongue. She moaned because, holy hell, she was about to…

Robin squeezed her eyes shut. *Oh my God…*

"Ah," she screamed.

She pressed her head against the couch cushion

and cried out again from the depths of her throat. The elusive vaginal orgasm. Dexter Frampton had given Robin her first.

AND NOW THEY WERE IN THE MASTER BEDROOM, IN bed. Dexter had the amazing ability to slow his thrusts so he could stave off his orgasm. He wanted making love to her to last. He'd waited too long for their first time for it to be over so soon. So finally, after coming, he collapsed, lying limp on top of her. Instead of asking him to get up so that she could be free of his heaviness, she wrapped her legs and arms around him, holding on tight.

Finally, Dexter rolled her, and she was lying on top of him.

"Fuck," he whispered. "Do you know how long I've been waiting to do that?"

She chuckled. "You've already told me, like about six times already."

He held her closer. "I hope this means you're giving me a chance to show you."

She was waiting on him to say more. "Show me what?" she finally asked.

"You should've picked me from the beginning.

All the time we wasted… We could've been doing this a year ago." His lips passionately kissed her forehead, and when she looked up at him, he planted one on the tip of her nose.

Robin closed her eyes to savor his tenderness. "Are you referring to Mars?" she asked breathlessly.

"He's fucking pathologically manipulative and selfish."

Robin agreed, but she remained silent. The thought made her cringe on the inside and not because Dexter was wrong. However, if Mars was as Dexter had defined him, then what did that say about her? Maybe she was deluding herself thinking she could ever deserve a sexy and normal guy like the demigod she'd just made real love to.

"What are you thinking?" Dexter asked.

Apparently, she had been quiet for too long. "So, um, how long do you plan on avoiding the media?" She chose not to address her insecurity, which probably would've made him run for the hills faster than expected.

Dexter chuckled nervously. It was something about him that she'd noticed, the nervous chuckle. "Are you planning on getting rid of me already?"

"No," she said without pause.

"Good."

"But you can avoid the vultures for now, but they will catch up with you at some point. I mean, Raymond Harrison is your father?" She snorted facetiously. "All that fucking family-first talk. I saw his con job a million miles away." Suddenly, Robin felt remorseful saying that about Dexter's biological father. "Sorry. He's your father. I should respect that."

He rubbed her arm gently. "It's not a problem. But Ray loved my mother, though. Still does. But family duty comes before a fashion model from Brooklyn."

She lifted her head off his chest. "Is that so?"

"Yes, babe."

Robin shook her head. "No, no, no. Too early for 'babe.'"

Dexter laughed. "Just testing the waters."

She rolled off of him and onto her back, resting her head on the fluffy pillow. "You know I'm fucked up, right?"

"No one goes through childhood unscathed, Robin."

She closed her eyes to ponder what she already knew. "Yeah… I know."

"But everybody doesn't deal with their shit.

Remember that dinner party at the Lords'?" he asked.

"I can't forget it. You were pretty hard on me."

"I apologize for that, babe… I mean Robin. Are we starting whatever this is we have between us in complete honesty?"

She turned to look at him. "I wouldn't have it any other way."

"I sensed you were hiding your fears behind a bloated sense of intellectual superiority."

Robin frowned. "No, I wasn't." She sounded as though she were whining.

"I didn't think you noticed it. But instead of being empathetic, I called you out on it in the wrong way. Then I did it again at the engagement party slash wedding."

"Right." She nudged him playfully on the side of his chest. "I forgot about that. I remember you dancing with all those women. Then Shawn Wright practically fucked you on the dance floor." She had been jealous, very jealous, watching the woman roll her bony ass against Dexter's crotch and him not stopping her. "I mean, the way she was dancing didn't fit the music." Robin shook her head. "Shameless."

Dexter was smiling from ear to ear. "I made you jealous."

Robin rolled her eyes. "No," she lied.

His lips found hers. "Just so you know, that was my intention," he said after the quick kiss.

"That's high school."

"I know. But you were driving me fucking crazy. I asked you to dance first, and—"

"I said no."

"So why did you say no?"

Robin groaned and folded her arms over her eyes. "Because."

Dexter carefully unfolded her arms. "I get you, Robin. I really do. I've been working with Sonja for a while. I know your shit. But more importantly, I know you better than you think. The inadequacy you feel about yourself is only in your head. And I'm going to still be around you when you finally get that and long after."

She stared at him, feeling her eyes water. "Do you mean that?" The words escaped her in a whisper.

"I do, Robin." He kissed her. "I do." He rolled himself on top of her.

They kissed, touched, rubbed, and kept it going

until he was ready for a very long session of round two.

Robin and Dexter could not stop making love. They did it for the rest of the day and all through the night, and they were still in bed the next day. Earlier, Dexter had left her to make two cheese omelets, though. They needed the fuel to make love a seventh time. Then Robin made coffee and warmed a few bagels so they could have enough energy to do it again.

They talked a lot too. He told her the story of why he and his ex-wife had divorced and how effectively they parented together. Robin wasn't even distracted by his fingers sliding up and down her wetness. Not anymore. He couldn't keep his hands off her, nor she him.

"She said something that got to you earlier while you were on the phone. What did she say?"

He smiled. "You read my expression?"

Robin could feel her face beam with a warmth and acceptance she'd never experienced before her encounter with Dexter. "Mm-hmm," she said, freely showing him the softer side of her.

"She advised me to not run and hide."

"And are you going to take her advice?"

"I'm not hiding, Robin. I'm keeping a low profile while my father's handlers contain the possible fallout."

Robin snorted. "Possible fallout? This guy's house of cards is going to come tumbling down." She closed her eyes and grunted gravely. "Sorry about that. He is your father."

"He's not a bad guy, Robin."

"How can you say that when he denied you?"

"He didn't deny privately. Ray's an unfortunate victim of his circumstances."

Robin twisted her face, showcasing her cynical thoughts. "Give me a break. And you call him Ray?"

Dexter turned to lie on his side, propping his head up with his hand. "Life isn't black and white, Robin. I thought you knew that. I've heard you defend the shades of gray in the past."

She sighed firmly. "It's not that. Ray put himself out there as the perfect Puritan. Yet here he is with a son who he loves in the shadows because he thinks people will judge him for it. You're his shame, Dexter. Doesn't that piss you off?"

"It used to. When I was eleven, I was messing up in school, testing my power. My mother sent me to camp, which was my father's apple orchard in Vermont."

Robin listened attentively as Dexter recalled how on day one, Raymond sat him down in the kitchen and frankly said, "I'm your father."

Then Raymond Harrison had started from the beginning, setting up the day he'd met Cherry Frampton, the beautiful fashion model from Brooklyn, New York. He was still in law school at Yale but had taken a trip from New Haven, Connecticut to the city to see what the hoopla was all about. Harrison laid eyes on Cherry while she was doing a photo shoot in the subway. He'd never seen such a beautiful woman, so brave and not like any woman he'd ever known. He waited until her shoot was over and asked her out for coffee. Cherry said yes, but instead of coffee, she took Ray out for jerk chicken in Queens and a dance hall party afterward. For two days straight, she guided him through New York, showing him the time of his life, and introduced him to people he never thought existed in real life. She said her goal was to melt his vanilla coating. By day three, after making love to her in the wee hours of the morning in Sheep's Meadow, he told her he wanted to spend the rest of his life with her.

But Ray and Cherry both knew that was merely a fantasy. He was from a family with a long political lineage and was being groomed to be the next president of the United States, and she was the wrong everything. So for one more week, the two had decided to live as though they would love each other for the rest of their lives.

"He told you that?" Robin asked.

"Yes, he did," Dexter said.

"And you were only eleven?"

"My mother and father always believed a person was never too young to handle the truth."

Robin sat up straight. "Wait a minute. Are they still involved?"

Dexter went on to explain how when he was eleven, that was his father's last summer as a single man. Harrison's family had pressured him to marry the current first lady, Laurelyn Harrison.

"Look up WASP in the dictionary, and there she'd be, waving at us," Robin said.

Dexter smiled mildly. "She's actually a very interesting person."

Robin could hardly believe that. "Then she knows about you?"

"Yes. She does."

"Was she forced to marry him?"

"Yes, she was."

"Ah." Robin nodded as though she understood clearly. "One thing I've learned about humans is we will always find a way to empower ourselves if someone tries to take it away. So Ray and Laurelyn have been getting over on the system that put them together ever since, huh?"

Dexter watched Robin with stars in his eyes.

"What?" she finally asked, simpering from his daze.

"That's one of the things that drew me to you— your ability to see beneath the surface."

"Oh." She rolled her eyes dismissively. "That depends on whether or not it's my life on the examination table. But you never answered—are your mother and the president still involved?"

Dexter put a hand on her knee. "If I tell you this, it stays in this room." He tilted his head in a manner that required her to say something.

"Of course," she said.

"My mother and father are legally married to each other."

"But what about the first lady?"

"Laurelyn Harrison isn't married to anyone."

Robin's mouth dropped. She had been privy to a lot of salacious shit in the past, but what Dexter had just told her took the cake. "Wow," Robin said. "How the hell did this cat get out of the bag?"

"Jessica St. James."

"Right," Robin said. "She's a manipulative little thing."

"She tried to give me a blow job in exchange for a role on *Pact of Lies*, and when I turned her down, she threatened to expose my secret. I called her bluff, thinking she really didn't have anything on me." He sniffed. "I was wrong."

Robin took his hand and held it tightly. "I'm sorry this happened to you and your family. But you know what? We live in different times now. People are begging for our politicians to stop taking the fucking money and be honest with us, tell us what they truly stand for, who they really are, show us that we're all human together. You know?"

Dexter stared at her with that admiring grin again. Then he leaned forward to gently kiss her lips. Once they started, they couldn't stop, and soon, they were making love until they both climaxed.

CHAPTER 10

*T*he next day, Robin had received an express-mail package that was addressed to her from Luddie. She and the girls had gone to Dexter's townhome to pack more things for a long stay away from home. In the process, she'd packed clothes, daily essentials, files for projects Dexter was in the middle of working on, and his MacBook Pro. Luddie had also reported that the photographers had still been camped outside on his steps when she'd arrived, but she had called her husband, Patrick, who was a New York police detective, and he'd sent someone out to clear away the vultures for loitering. She and the girls had left once they were gone. Robin was impressed by how Dexter and his ex-wife were more than just friends; they were family.

Dexter had also been in touch with his mother by use of a secure line. They'd been planning their next step. Meanwhile, shortly after Dexter's package arrived, Robin received her delivery of wires, glass, plastics, metals, ladders, a few platforms, hooks, soldering gun, a welding helmet, and other necessities required to complete her installation project. It had been quite a while since she'd felt so inspired. It was as if ideas were falling into her brain like binary code dropping from the sky. Her every decision made sense.

Days passed into night, and pretty soon, they were into the second week of hibernating in their love cave. At times, Dexter would enter her studio and bring her a sandwich or bagel or another cup of coffee. Mostly when he came into her workspace, they would end up making love on the chaise that faced the view of the East River. Sometimes, he would come just to taste her, and when she took a break, she would go into the office where he worked so she could put her mouth on him.

She loved how he listened to her explain in detail her ideas about moving forward in her project. He would ask her questions like "How did you come to that conclusion?" When she would play him parts of her installation and ask how it made him feel, he would tug her against him, and his passionate kiss would be the answer.

It was twenty minutes after noon on a Wednesday, or maybe Thursday, when Robin's cell phone rang. She was in the middle of testing a light effect, but her gut told her it was Claudia checking in, so she quickly answered.

Robin tapped her earpod, and it picked up the call. "Yes, Claudia, you can view the first segment by this weekend."

There was a brief silence, and then a male voice said, "Hi."

Robin stiffened. "Mars?"

"How have you been?" he asked as though he were catching up with an old friend.

"What do you want?" she snapped.

"Ah, I see. You know what was between Plume and I wasn't real, right?"

"Hey babe, come here!" Dexter called from the den, where he'd been watching television.

Robin looked over her shoulder. "Lose my number," she said quickly then ended the call. She had to control her anger as she stomped up the hallway to see what Dexter wanted. There was no way she was going to tell him Mars had just called. That man had a lot of nerve contacting her. Over the last few months, she'd come to realize Mars had embarrassed and devalued her more than he'd broken her heart. Robin heard her phone ringing in the distance, but as she got closer to the den, the sound of the television overtook Mars's second call.

Dexter was sitting on the sofa, watching a news report on BCN.

"What's going on?" she asked, narrowing her eyes at the TV.

He quickly looked back at her then waved her over. "Come here."

Robin kept her eyes on the screen as she sat on his lap. A beautiful older woman with caramel skin and the same light-blue eyes she had basked in hundreds of times while gazing at Dexter was being interviewed.

"Is that your mom?" Robin asked.

"Yeah." He kept his eyes fixed on his mother's face.

The crawl beneath the shot of Cherry Frampton defined her as a world-famous fashion model and long-time mistress of President Raymond Harrison. She was being questioned about her relationship with the president.

"And of course you're here speaking for President Harrison and the first lady," Jack Crossly, BCN's most popular reporter, said.

Robin gasped. "They're telling the truth?"

Dexter held her tighter. "I convinced them to follow your advice."

Ripping her gaze away from the extremely beautiful Cherry Frampton to fix her eyes on Dexter felt like looking away from a train wreck. "What are you talking about?"

Dexter did a better job of talking to her while keeping his stare fastened on his mother. "Remember when you said we live in a different world and people will appreciate the truth?"

"I remember saying something like that."

"I talked to Mother and tried to convince her to tell the truth. I think I got through to her."

"Wow. That's brave but perhaps kamikaze as well." She refocused on the interview. If Cherry Frampton and Raymond Harrison told the truth, all hell would break loose.

"I know," Dexter muttered.

"Then please, Ms. Frampton, tell the world the nature of your relationship with the president."

Cherry appeared unfazed by the phrasing of

the question, which was designed to support a sensationalistic headline.

"They're savvy with their bullshit, aren't they?" Robin asked, maintaining laser focus on the television screen.

Dexter grunted in a way that said he agreed.

"When Raymond and I were young, we fell in love. We had a child."

"Well, one that he never claimed, mind you."

"He's always claimed our son."

"Your son is Dexter Frampton, one of the biggest producers in Hollywood?"

"I am?" Dexter asked.

"You are now," Robin replied.

They both snorted sarcastically.

"Our son is very successful, and we're both proud of him."

"Thanks, Mom," Dexter said to the image on the TV.

"He's a Hollywood elite, though. I'm pretty sure Harrison and his supporters—"

"Jack, my son lives in Brooklyn, and you know that. Furthermore, Raymond has never used that term. Now, I'm not saying those who support him haven't."

"I can assure you that they certainly have," Jack Crossly said with a straight face.

"Well, as you know, this political business can get quite dicey. Raymond knew when he was very young what was expected of him, the tangled web of, um… expectations. He could've done three things, Jack."

"Other than tell the truth about having a son out of wedlock and then running a campaign based on family values?" Crossly asked.

"Yes, other than that."

"Is there anything other than that?"

Cherry narrowed her eyes at Jack. "Can I ask you something?"

"Ask away."

She leaned toward Jack Crossly. "What are family values exactly?"

Crossly pressed his lips together.

"I venture to say that the sad fact is that he loved me dearly, but those who inflicted their family values on him made him deny what he felt and fulfill their expectations. I have a son. I knew very early in his life that he needed nothing more than my love and attention. It's such a powerful role for a human to take on, parent. We know we've made mistakes, Raymond and I, but we love our son. And there's no way in hell we are not going to love him because Raymond's family had expectations."

A look of admiration came over Jack Crossly. "Cherry, well said. I'm glad you were on my show. Good luck with the fallout. You're a class act, but this isn't going to go down easy for Harrison's supporters or detractors."

Cherry said nothing but smiled humbly as Crossly took them to break. Dexter used the remote control to turn off the television. They sat in silence for a few beats.

"Your mother is amazing," Robin said.

He smiled proudly. "I know."

"Hey, so does this mean we can go out to dinner tonight?"

Dexter planted an unexpected kiss on her lips. She could feel him growing hard beneath her.

"How about we order in tonight and go out tomorrow night?" His hand slid under the hem of her dress and up her thigh until he found that sensitive spot.

Robin gasped and moaned. It was a direct hit. She'd stopped wearing panties days ago due to the fact that Dexter was always taking them off. She was breathing heavily through her nose as pleasurable sensations flooded her pussy.

The doorbell rang, bringing sobriety to the moment.

"To be continued," Dexter whispered.

Robin swallowed the lump in her throat and nodded. "I'll get it," she said after she found her voice.

She tried to leap to her feet, but he pulled her back down onto his lap. "The cat's already out of the bag, babe."

Robin kissed him, and her head spun like usual. "Then let's go answer the door together," she said breathlessly.

They leered at each other. That was how it was with Dexter—Robin could actually feel the molecules of attraction swirling around them. She breathed them in. They saturated her insides and filled her soul.

The doorbell rang again. They stood together. Dexter put his arm around her waist, and they walked together. It felt freeing to finally let someone see them as a couple. The only people who knew they were officially making a go at a relationship were Sonja, Jay, and Vincent Adams, the president and owner of the media company where Dexter was president of original content.

Dexter looked through the peephole then frowned as if he'd drunk a cup of hot vinegar.

"What the hell?" he whispered as he turned the locks and opened the door.

Two burly men in black suits stood side by side. "Mr. Frampton?" one of them asked.

"I know who you are," he said.

The men kept expressionless faces. "Will you please come with us?"

Robin turned her wide-eyed expression to Dexter.

"They're Secret Service," he said.

Her mouth fell open.

CHAPTER 11

THREE DAYS LATER

*R*obin had just ended her customary morning call with Dexter, although talking to him on the telephone didn't seem sufficient enough. It was weird because she'd spent most of her adulthood living alone, yet his absence had left a big, gaping hole in her life.

One thing about the Secret Service—they were efficient. Dexter had packed fast. His family was lying low until the White House could get a handle on the fallout from the shit storm Jessica St. James had started all because Dexter had refused to give her a role on a television show. During the conversation Robin had had with him that morning, Dexter had admitted Jessica wasn't a bad actress.

Actually, she was a better actress than singer, but she'd disqualified herself from landing the role when she'd tried to give him a blow job. Dexter had been around Hollywood a long time, and he was tired of women licking, sucking, and fucking their way to their next big break and not being called out for it.

"I should've taken her seriously. As mildly talented as she is, she didn't get that far by making empty threats," he had said regarding Jessica. "But all I could think about was living in a world where my daughters could get away with the same kind of dastardly shit she tried on me. We teach them to use their minds, intellect, and charm, not their pussies."

Regardless, he had to accept the shoes he was standing in and try to make the best of them. He and Robin would see each other in seven days. Before agreeing to go with the strapping men in suits, he'd called his mother and told her that he would only hide out for ten days. After that, he would have to resume his life. Dexter had a lot of new TV projects in the works. Truth be told, he would soon have to abandon their love nest and fly to Vancouver to help manage the production budget crisis for *Pact of Lies*. Three days down, seven more to go. The wait felt like an eternity.

Robin reached for the remote control on the nightstand and turned on the television. The channel was already set to BCN as it had been for the last three days. President Harrison's approval rating had taken a nosedive. Even though it was his second term, the sparring opposition party was demanding an impeachment hearing. The purists were out in force, railing about how the president had lied and if it weren't for his stance on family values, he would've never won. It was all the same manufactured outrage and bullshit Robin and the rest of the country had become familiar with when it came to politics. She sighed with an eye roll, turned off the television, slid out of bed, and got ready to finally show a portion of her project to Claudia, who was scheduled to arrive soon.

THE BLACKOUT SHADES WERE OVER THE WINDOWS. Robin stood by the door, watching Claudia examine her creation. All that could be heard were Claudia's tiny heels tapping the concrete floor as she viewed the installation from all angles. At certain times, she would stop to look at a section of the installations as though she were transfixed by it.

"Let me know if you have any questions," Robin said.

Claudia waved a hand, shushing her. After a moment, she spread her fingers over her heart. "My God, Robin. What a way to redeem yourself. I'm in love."

Robin smiled. "Thanks. I'm happy you love it."

"No." Claudia shook her head empathically. "I mean this is love. I'm in love with something. I don't know what because this makes me feel that way."

Robin frowned dubiously. "Is that so?"

"I have a question for you," Claudia said, viewing the installation as though it would hurt to look away.

Robin walked over and stood beside her. "I'm listening."

"Are you in love?"

She turned her head slightly. "Why do you ask that?"

Claudia put an arm around Robin's waist. "I don't think you've really appreciated my talent."

"Yes, I have."

"No, you haven't. You think I'm a phony with a phony accent. And wear too much makeup, have too much hair, and only care about making celebrities your fans. Am I wrong?"

Robin pressed her lips together, pondering Claudia's accusation. "Well, I don't think you have too much hair."

Claudia affectionately squeezed Robin's waist. "Thank you. I like my hair. It would kill me if you didn't."

They chuckled.

"Here's why I asked if you're in love. In Soulscape Part One, I saw two elements—the shame that makes you believe you're unlovable and your longing for the man with light in his eyes."

Robin's mouth fell open as she turned to Claudia, who had just voiced what Robin knew but couldn't put into words.

Claudia smirked and winked at her. "Do you have a whole new appreciation for me now?"

She smiled gently. "I do."

"Is it Dexter?"

"We're in a relationship, yes." She kept her tone pragmatic.

"And you love him?" Claudia tilted her head in a way that urged Robin not to lie to her.

So Robin closed her eyes and let her heart answer. "I think I've loved him from the first time I saw him. At least my soul did."

Claudia squeezed her waist again. "Good girl,

Robin Hester. I know that was hard for you to admit."

Silence fell as Robin considered what Claudia had just said. For the first time ever, she viewed her own art as a spectator. She skipped a breath. It was his eyes. It was her heart. It was the fiery lust and the passionate love between them. All along, he had been her inspiration.

"So what are you doing for lunch?" Robin asked, still choked up.

"Eating with you," Claudia said.

"Then let's go eat."

"Do you know this is the first time you've ever asked me to have a meal with you?"

Robin jerked her head. "No way." She tried to think of instances in which she'd asked Claudia to eat with her but couldn't recall any. "Oh my God, you're right."

Claudia raised a finger. "And for the record, my accent is real. It's just not one thing or the other."

Robin narrowed an eye at Claudia. "Are you sticking to that story?"

After a moment, Claudia rolled her eyes. "Okay, but don't tell anyone," she said in perfect American English.

Robin tossed her head and laughed. She was doing that often lately, laughing. A certain happiness resided in her these days, an emotion that had always eluded her.

BEING DWARFED BY MAZES OF BRICK BUILDINGS AND walking on the overburdened sidewalks and past piles of trash lined up along the edge of the sidewalk didn't bother Robin anymore. She wasn't sure whether that was a good or bad thing. Thinking about home left a bitter taste in her mouth. Mars lived in LA. Gran had moved to the desert. These days, Sonja and Elaine were hardly ever in the city. They spent a lot of time in their new husbands' homes away from home. And Theresa lived in Seattle, although Robin wasn't sure whether her sister liked living there or not. Terry had always done a pretty good job of convincing everyone that she was "pumped up, energized, and ready to kick some ass" as she always said. Perhaps the time had come for Robin to change it up and move to a different town.

She and Claudia went to a restaurant in the

Empire Stores marketplace. Robin had actually ordered their food often but always to go. That afternoon, she was actually sitting down and having a meal.

"You seem comfortable getting from point A to point B," Claudia said. "Have you and Dexter been enjoying your new neighborhood?" Her squinted eyes twinkled.

Robin simpered as she looked down. "What makes you think Dexter's been with me?"

"I put one and one together and came out with two."

"Meaning?" Robin asked.

Claudia bounced in her seat then scooted to the edge of her chair. "Well, last week BCN said that he was hiding out at Camp David with the rest of the family. But after I saw your installation and you admitted that you've fallen in love with him, then I suspected he was actually hiding out with you. You can't fall in love with someone who hasn't been around you. So is he still at your place?"

Robin smirked. "You're so clever, aren't you?"

Claudia's smile expanded. "Then he's at your place this very minute?"

Robin checked over her shoulder to make sure

no one was listening to them. No one was. It was New York; everyone was used to minding their own business. "He was." She took care to keep her voice down. "Secret Service collected him three days ago."

"Wow, you're a lucky duckling. He's so perfect."

She was ready to say that no one was perfect, but Dexter may have really been perfect. The fact that he loved her and had been making love to her was surreal.

Of course Claudia had to direct their focus back to work. The woman was a serious workaholic, probably more of one than Robin had ever been. When their food arrived, Claudia was telling her all about the local venue she was trying to land for the exhibit. The problem was that only local artists were allowed to show in their halls.

"Peter Canter will probably stop by your studio on Monday. He wants to make sure you're building your project in Brooklyn and that it's better than your showing in Berlin."

Robin snorted cynically. "So basically, he's quality control? He wants to see if part two of my installation isn't a"—she drew air quotes —"'Christmas lights project.'"

Claudia pushed her fingers toward Robin. "Don't take it personal. He's an arrogant asshole."

Robin nodded. "Right."

Perhaps it was the way the arugula sat on top of her turkey burger. Once upon a time, she'd managed a café that was owned by her aunt, Sonja and Elaine's mother, but Robin had abandoned it. She'd really enjoyed making the café a Sunday morning hotspot on the west side. So many times, she'd wanted to direct all her focus toward Brew & Bake, which was the name of the café. But by then, she was making income that exceeded a million a year on her art. Given enough time, she could've pulled that same income out of Brew & Bake. Perhaps the fact that it belonged to Carrie Anne put a bad taste in her mouth. After the establishment was sold, Carrie Anne had contacted Gran and asked for the proceeds. The only reason Robin had found out was because Nigel, her accountant, had told her in confidence.

"What are you thinking, Robin?"

Robin opened her mouth to answer the question, but Claudia's phone rang. After seeing who was calling, her manager said, "I have to take this." She got up, holding the device against her ear.

Robin kept her gaze on Claudia until she

walked out the door. "I'm done," she said to herself. "After this exhibit, it's over."

"That's too bad," a familiar voice said.

She quickly turned to see who was standing behind her. Her eyes expanded, and her heart tightened at the sight of Mars MacAvoy.

CHAPTER 12

*H*e kissed her on the mouth before she saw it coming.

"What are you doing here?" she asked, pressing her fingers against her lips.

Mars picked up the chair Claudia had abandoned and set it down next to Robin, blocking her escape path. Then he sat, and his face was uncomfortably close.

"I miss you," he whispered thickly.

She leaned away from him, noticing the pure lust in his eyes. "I'm confused." Her gaze veered down to his left ring finger. "I thought you were marrying Plume." He wasn't wearing a ring.

"Did I tell you that?" His tone was sharp.

"No, but it was reported in the media."

"But did I tell you that?"

Mars always had the ability to make her uneasy at the drop of a hat. She wanted to fight back because she truly understood his manipulative game.

"Of course you never told me about your relationship with Plume. That would require a lot more integrity than you have."

She was familiar with his arrogant smile. Normally, she would look away from it for some reason, but this time she couldn't. There it was for her viewing displeasure, the truth of who he was so up close and personal.

"Come on. When did you starting believing that shit? You know I have people handling me."

His face was still too close for comfort, so she leaned back even more. "I saw you."

"You saw me?"

She folded her arms. "I saw you and Plume fucking."

Mars narrowed his eyes. "And I know you've been fucking Dexter Frampton." He set his jaw as though her relationship with Dexter justified his betrayal.

Robin wanted to laugh in his face, but that

wasn't her style, nor was arguing with him about a situation that was a lost cause.

"What are you doing here?" she asked. "For real. What are you doing here?"

"I'm here for you."

"But you already know Dexter and I are together. By the way, who told you?"

He shrugged nonchalantly. "Who gives a fuck?"

Robin shot to her feet. "Okay, I'm leaving."

Mars took her hand. "Sit down." His eyes softened in a way she'd never seen before. "Please."

Robin cautiously sat back down.

"I saw the two of you together," Mars said. "When I came to your hotel room a few weeks ago. I went to explain my situation between Plume and I then."

Her eyes narrowed to slits, and she stretched her neck forward. "I. Do. Not. Believe. You."

"I love you. I always have, and I'm ready to go public with it."

"I walked into your house and to your favorite room and saw you fucking Plume. That was back in August. We're in December. It took you this long to see the light on loving me?"

He sighed sharply. "I don't know what to say to

you other than I'm disappointed that you landed in Frampton's bed."

His words made such an impact on Robin that she closed her eyes to absorb them. Now Mars showing up out of nowhere made sense. He'd always had a spiteful and vengeful thirteen-year-old boy living inside him.

"He told me about Sandy Deleon," Robin said.

Mars watched her, expressionless. Then out of nowhere, he pulled her against him. His tongue made it only halfway into her mouth before she shoved him in the chest. She wiped her mouth with the back of her hand as she watched him storm toward the exit.

He passed Claudia, who took a step back to watch him push the glass door and continue on his way.

She tilted her head slightly as she walked back to the table. "What the hell happened?"

Robin was still breathing fire, but she couldn't stop shaking her head because indeed that was the answer to Claudia's question. "I have no idea what that was all about. None whatsoever."

Robin waited for her phone to ring. Two days had gone by, and she hadn't heard from Dexter. She made sure she kept her cell phone with her at all times, even when she went to the bathroom. For the most part, she was spending most of her day in the studio, putting the final touches on the installation project. She even tweaked here and there, allowing her heart to guide her. It hadn't taken long to put Mars's strange visit out of her mind. He was merely a spoiled and entitled man who always had a major problem forgiving those who bruised his ego. It was clear to Robin that Mars had never forgiven and forgotten Dexter for threatening to turn him into the authorities for being sexually aggressive with the underage Sandy Deleon. Once again, Mars's grand gesture of affection wasn't about loving her; it was about loving himself.

Robin climbed down from the ladder, turned the lights off, then stood back to admire her handi-work. After absorbing an eyeful, she smiled. She had done well.

Her cell phone rang just as the doorbell buzzed. She was expecting Claudia and Peter Cantor. They were supposed to view the final project for approval to show at the local venue. They could wait. Two days of not hearing Dexter say "I love you" felt like an eternity. Something in her heart told her that it was him on the phone.

"Hello," she said.

"What the hell's going on with you?" It was her sister.

"Terry?"

"Are you really back with Mars MacAvoy?"

"What?"

The doorbell rang again, and Robin glanced over her shoulder.

"That woman on the early-morning gossip show, can't think of her name, but I'm surfing through channels this morning, and there's your photo with a caption that read, 'This artist gets around.'"

Another call buzzed. Robin drew the phone away from her ear to see the caller. It was Sonja. Apparently, all hell was breaking loose. The doorbell rang again, and she suddenly felt as though she were trapped in indecision.

CHAPTER 13

DEXTER FRAMPTON

Two Days Ago

Before that morning, Dexter had planned to leave and head back to Brooklyn to be with Robin. DUMBO was nice, but he was ready to have her in his home in Greenpoint. He was ready for Mariana and Maribel to meet her and to fall in love with her uniqueness just as he had. His daughters were great in that way. They gravitated toward the unconventional. After he washed his face, brushed his teeth, and put on fresh clothes, Dexter headed to the sunroom to inform his mother of his decision to leave.

The first day he'd spent at the Harrison Family Orchard Estate in Vermont, his mother had asked to hear all about Robin. He'd started from the very first time he'd laid eyes on her at Jay's house. He had opened the front door, and there stood the one.

"When she's not with me, I walk around with a big, gaping hole in my heart," the president had said regarding his mother. Thirty-six years later, that hadn't changed.

Cherry was happy for Dexter and couldn't wait to meet Robin. Not long after Dexter settled in, Amy Harrison showed up. The world knew her as the president and first lady's daughter, but she wasn't related to Dexter by blood, which meant she wasn't Ray's daughter. Her father was a man named Douglas Roth, an army general who'd served under three presidents and was still working in the Harrison White House. Amy never acknowledged Doug Roth as anything more than a liar. She was the sort of person who had agreed to keep her parents' secrets, but not a day went by when she didn't make them pay for them in one form or another.

Dexter had no doubt Amy would be sequestered. She was unpredictable. Last year, she was a contestant on *Safe House*, a reality TV show in which houseguests voted a person out each week and the winner was the last girl or guy standing. She continuously sought the spotlight. For the right sort of exposure, she would sell out Ray and Laurelyn, which was why even during Ray's terms as a senator, Amy had had a regular security detail. At first, they were all men, but she would end up seducing and fucking them to get her way. Her new security detail consisted of three women. They were referred to as her media team, but in fact, they were twenty-four-hour-a-day babysitters.

Amy was twenty-seven years old with the aptitude of a sixteen-year-old spoiled girl. Dexter couldn't count the times Amy had tried to sneak into his bed or slide into the shower with him. She was obsessed with him. When she'd heard him tell Cherry about his new girlfriend, Amy's face turned red, then she had stomped out of the room.

For the last three days, her media team had been keeping her busy, tracking all the news stories in which her name was mentioned and figuring out how to capitalize on all of the publicity in the future. Dexter would only see her at dinner. During the day, he video-conferenced into all his meetings and previewed completed projects among other things. The only time he didn't occupy himself with work was during his phone calls with Robin, which had become his lifeline. He had just ended his two-hour call with Robin. The time went by way too fast. But she had revealed that she was a hundred percent certain Soulscape Part Two would be her last art project. She was done. However, she had no idea what to do next. He didn't want to abandon Robin during her time of confusion. Yep, he would leave. And the first person he needed to talk to about it was Cherry.

He cupped his hands around his mouth and blew nervously into them. His heart pounded like thunder as he headed down the long hallway. Cherry was out front, directing staff on how to decorate the exterior of the mansion for Christmas. Or she could've been in the kitchen, making sure lunch was prepared to her standards. So far, he'd missed every sit-down lunch gathering, and Cherry hadn't been happy about it. But that day, since he was leaving, he planned to make his mother happy by joining the family at the table.

"Robin Hester," he heard Amy say.

He stopped in his tracks then turned to see her smirking in the grand den. She was lying across the big sofa, so he could only see her head from where he stood, that was until she crossed her bare legs on the back of the sofa.

"She has a new boyfriend, Dexie," she said.

Dexter ignored the jab she took at him and narrowed his eyes at the television. The video had been halted as though Amy had it set and ready for him to view. Then it played.

He felt as if he were blinking in slow motion as he watched a clip of a cell phone video that captured Robin and Mars MacAvoy kissing, not once, but twice. The second kiss was longer, more passionate. It was the kiss that convinced him Robin was back under Mars's spell. The host of the show, Bobbie Smith, was giving her opinion on Robin being the kind of woman who liked powerful men in Hollywood.

"Oh, and this part is about us," Amy said during a brief pause.

"There's a rumor about Dexter Frampton." Bobbie Smith leaned in the opposite direction of the camera to speak to someone offstage. "Is it still a rumor?"

The person said something to her, and then she settled more comfortably in her seat. "It's not a rumor. Well, Dexter Frampton is a famous Hollywood producer and writer." She went on to list the movies he had written and the TV series he'd created. "So yeah, he's a big deal in Hollywood," she said to the audience as if she were letting them in on a secret. Then she sat back in her seat and slouched. "Get ready for this. He's also President Raymond Harrison's illegitimate son." The audience gasped, but she waved them silent. "But that's not all. So this is Dexter Frampton."

Dexter's picture filled the screen. He remembered that shot. It was his first Academy Award nomination and red-carpet appearance for his screenplay *The Love of a Bad Man*. He hadn't won. The audience catcalled and cheered. "Oh yes, Bobbie," they said as though she were gossiping with old friends.

"He is drop-dead gorgeous," Bobbie continued. "Those eyes… But he doesn't get them from his father. His mother is Cherry Frampton." A photo of his mother appeared on the screen. It was from a few years ago when she did a campaign for aging beautifully. The audience oohed and aahed again.

Bobbie twisted around in her seat to get a good look of mother and son side by side. "Look at those genes. Stunningly gorgeous. But if you look closely, you can see that he also resembles the president. But she doesn't."

A picture of Amy was shown. It was from her reality show and wasn't a very flattering one. But by the gleam in her eyes when she looked at Dexter,

Amy wasn't aware of Bobbie and her production staff's tactics. It was their way of separating Amy, who was quite an attractive woman, from Dexter and his mother. Basically, Bobbie Smith was about to drop the hammer, and Dexter knew exactly what she was going to say next.

"Now give us a side-by-side of the 'siblings.'" Bobbie drew air quotes around that last word. She studied the photos of Dexter and Amy. "They are not related. Now show Amy and her mother." The images changed. "Get a good look. Now Amy and the president."

The audience rumbled.

"Okay!" she said excitedly. "Then you see what I see." Bobbie folded her arms and twisted her mouth. The audience laughed. "And now one political party is calling for him to quit the presidency, and the other party is trying to convince us that it's not true. But the proof is in the receipts."

Now all their photos were on the screen—Amy, Laurelyn, Cherry, Dexter, Ray, and a black box with a question mark in the center.

"Now, who's the missing baby daddy?"

Amy shot to her feet then stretched seductively. She was wearing shorts so short that they resembled panties and a tiny halter top. "I have the answer they're looking for. You think she'll invite me on the show if I promise to tell her?"

Dexter shook his head and was on the verge of talking his silly sister-by-association away from the neon lights of five minutes of fame.

"Now, getting back to this one…" Bobbie pointed at a picture of Robin. "No, the other one. The kiss."

Dexter clenched his fists as his stomach turned. He'd seen and heard enough, so he stomped off. Dexter didn't know where he was going from there. He didn't want to go back to New York after seeing that kiss. Robin's lips had belonged to him before seeing that clip.

"Dexie." Amy's voice echoed through the hallway.

He stopped abruptly and, without really thinking about it, turned around. "What?"

She was posing against the wall, pushing her fake tits out, and curving her back with one foot against the wall. "Let's fuck, finally. I'm yours. Take me any way you want. Pound me to get back at the fucking, cheating bitch."

Dexter sneered as he whipped himself around and continued walking with no destination in mind. He knew that he didn't want to see his mother. She would pick up on his mood and keep on him until he divulged what was upsetting him. Then he had an idea.

He went in the opposite direction to the office he'd been working in to call Sonja and ask if it were true. She would know. Robin told her everything. After flopping down on the big black leather chair, he picked up his cell phone, but it didn't have a signal. Next, he tried the office phone, but it was also dead. His computer didn't have internet access.

"Fuck!" he shouted at the top of his lungs.

Amy appeared in the doorway, completely naked. "I'm ready," she purred.

Dexter smashed his hands over his face and groaned with frustration. He was in hell, actual hell. "What the fuck is wrong with you?"

"Me? What the fuck is wrong with you? I can't believe you're going to keep rejecting me. I'm hot!"

He shook his head. "How old are you, sixteen?"

Amy recoiled. "It's just sex, Dexter. And what's wrong with me anyway? Why am I never good enough for you?"

And that was when it hit him. She kept trying because he kept rejecting her. Amy was simply replicating the relationship she had with her father, the elusive general. So, Dexter got up, took his overcoat off the coat-tree, and walked over to wrap it around her naked body.

"You know I love you, Amy," he said.

She stood very still.

"How long have I known you?"

"Why are you asking me that?" she asked briskly.

"Just answer. How long have we known each other?"

Her frown intensified. "Since we were kids."

"And I'm still here. In your life. I care about you a lot, enough to not give in to your crazy advances. You know me. You know I'm not the kind of guy who fucks just to fuck. You know this, and yet you're always coming for me. Have you ever asked yourself why you keep doing that?"

She took her frown up another notch then opened her mouth to speak but closed it again.

"Think about it," Dexter urged.

"My God! What are you trying to say, Dexter?"

"I'm saying that you get your kicks out of me rejecting you. It's your fucking self-fulfilling prophecy. If I were to have sex with you, it would feel like a violation because it would be one." He narrowed an eye. "Think about it."

"I am thinking about it." After a moment, she

clenched the opening of the jacket tighter. "What are you saying?" she whispered.

"You know, they never really put you in therapy because they were afraid of what you would say to the doctor. Your mother and my dad and my mom and your dad have always protected their lies over our fucking sanity. And I'm saying, Amy, the reason why your life is a constant state of rejection—either it's a reality show, or another loser boyfriend, or you coming on to me—is because it's where you're comfortable. You've felt rejected your whole life. And it's about time you work on feeling wanted."

Amy's eyes narrowed then expanded then tapered again. "Fuck you, Dexter," she hissed before stomping off.

He stood there in front of the desk, pondering what had just happened. Amy had become collateral damage because of their family secrets and perpetual lies. Standing there, he suddenly felt as though going along with his parents' and the first lady's plan didn't seem reasonable. When he was married to Luddie, he'd always felt like a liar for keeping such an earth-shattering secret from the mother of his daughters. Perhaps it was because he knew Luddie wouldn't have been so gracious about it. She would've confronted Cherry and perhaps spoken to the press for the purpose of the greater good.

Dexter turned and glowered at his desk. He had to do something. Amy had never stripped naked and begged him to fuck her. She was coming unhinged. And he had always been the good boy, the one who so diligently kept the lies so as not to harm his mother and father. It wasn't right. He had to do something, and he had to do it for that greater good Luddie had always believed in.

Dexter checked the time on his watch. It was a couple of minutes after noon. Dave, who worked in the vinegar mill, would be making his customary run to the Harrison Farm Café and Country Store soon. Dexter had had a long conversation with Dave on the day he'd arrived. The organic apple vinegar, a fairly new product they'd started producing, had been flying off the shelves. He wanted to catch Dave before he made his next trip. Dexter rushed as fast as he could to the factory and took the back way so that he wouldn't run into Cherry.

Bright-green grass surrounded the mansion estate. Two large mills, a cider mill and a vinegar mill, were south of the main house. Rounding the estate and its structures were acres of apple trees, which were carefully nurtured all year long.

Dexter ran into Dave and two other men loading the truck before heading off the compound.

He waved. "Hey, Dave," he called from only a few feet away.

Dave waved back. "How's it going, Dexter?"

The guy was young, probably in his late twenties or early thirties, and had a genuine good-guy smile. Dexter walked up to him and slapped his hands together. *First things first.* "Hey, do you have a cell phone on you?"

He shrugged. "They collected all our phones at the gate."

Dexter knocked twice on the back of the small cargo truck. "Do they check what you have back here on the way out?"

"Only coming in," Dave said.

"Then can I catch a ride to the café?"

Dave studied him dubiously. The look on his face said he knew Dexter wasn't supposed to leave the compound. The scandal that had rocked the White House was known by most of the country. Everyone who worked on the property knew to keep their eyes and ears to themselves, as well as keep their mouths shut when it came to being questioned by outside sources. On top of that, no one had known much of anything about their family secrets before the recent blow-up. Cherry and Ray would only spend time together at the orchards during the off-season, and she would bring her own loyal house staff to look after their needs. But now everyone knew the family was hiding out. A huge security detail was posted at the gate and around the perimeter twenty-four hours a day.

Dexter stepped closer and whispered, "I'll pay you."

Dave held up a hand. "No need for that. A man is born free, so get in."

Dexter wanted to kiss the guy for not making him jump through his hoops. He climbed in the back of the small cargo truck with the boxes of vinegar and cider. Once they were all packed and ready to go, Dave pulled the door down and locked it, and soon they were rolling along. Dexter panicked some when the car stopped at the main gate.

"Back out again?" one of the guards asked.

"In and out," Dave said. "We do this all day!"

The guard laughed and told Dave that he would see him when he got back. And then the truck was rolling smoothly up Harrison Highway. Dexter thought about how his father's family owned the town. But then thoughts of Robin tried to take over.

He couldn't let that kiss she'd shared with Mars occupy his mind, at least not at the moment. Now that he'd had some time to cool off, he thought he owed himself the opportunity to listen to her explanation. If he'd had cell phone access, he would've called her to ask her what that kiss was all about. However, thinking about Mars's lips on hers made him want to tear the roof off the truck. Nope, Mars didn't deserve to kiss Robin, especially now that she belonged solely to him. He was going to rip the guy's head off the next time he saw him.

Dexter sighed sharply. "Shit," he muttered. Obsessing over Robin was not the reason he'd snuck into the uncomfortable and dark truck. His family needed the sort of help they hadn't known to ask for. They were getting clobbered by the media. His father's poll numbers had dropped to the lowest in history, all because Ray continued playing politics, and that wasn't good. Earlier, when Dexter studied Amy, he saw how far she had descended into the darkness that their lies had dragged her into. He was lucky —he had Cherry, who'd never put much before him besides keeping her relationship with her lover closeted for so many years. But Amy was raised by nannies and was only brought out of the box when she had to perform the daughter role for her parents. Dexter had always known the reason why Amy was so fucked up. Today, he decided to do something about it.

Soon, the truck stopped, the door rolled up, light flooded the cab, and he squinted.

DEXTER DIDN'T GO INTO THE CAFÉ. HE DIDN'T want anyone to know he was there. Instead, he walked a mile up the road and entered a real-estate office, which was owned by an old friend named James Wrightwood. He was rolling dice on whether James was in the office. Dexter smiled broadly when he looked across the room at the ruddy-faced guy with a deeply receding hairline, sitting in the only office in the building and behind the biggest desk.

"Dexie, is that you?" James asked.

Dexter held his arms out. "Jamie!"

They shook hands as they hugged.

"What the hell are you doing here?" his old friend asked.

"I need to use your phone." Dexter figured there was no time to sugarcoat the reason for his visit.

James leaned back. "My phone?"

"Yep. Your phone."

James studied him with a frown. "Is this about what's in the news?"

"It is."

After a moment, James patted Dexter on the back of his shoulder. "Brittany, get the man a phone."

A young woman in her early twenties, who had turned red in the face, couldn't stop smiling as she pointed at the phone in their small meeting room. Once Dexter was alone, he called Vincent Adams, who in turn called his wife, Maggie Adams. First, she agreed to hear him out, and after he filled her in on the details that she hadn't already heard in the news, she agreed to fly to Vermont immediately and meet with the family.

"You mean today?" Dexter was surprised by the swiftness with which she was ready to jump in and handle their problems.

"You want this handled?" she asked. There was an edge to her tone that made him forget to hesitate.

"Yes, I do."

"That's all you have to say. I'll see you and your family in three to four hours."

"Three to four hours?" That seemed fast. "My whole family isn't here."

"Don't worry. I'll handle that part. By the way, you're a smart guy, Dexter. I know you know Washington, D.C. isn't that different from Hollywood, and an average TV viewer is the spitting image of a voter. I've known you for a while. All the reasons my husband likes you as a colleague and a friend don't apply here. You have a lot of integrity, but in this case, the truth isn't going to set anyone free. Do you understand?"

Dexter closed his eyes and breathed in deeply through his nostrils. Maggie must've known he was riding high on ideals of a family living in the bliss of full disclosure. In a perfect world, *"We the people"* would understand what his mother had made him believe.

Ray couldn't defy his family to marry the one and only woman he could ever love and raise his only son due to obligations that went generations back. It wasn't the money or political power that made Ray toe the line; it was the possibility of losing the love of his parents, especially Rudolph Harrison, Dexter's ninety-five-year-old grandfather, who was still as mean as hell and controlling as ever. The only time that permanent frown on Ray's face was turned upside down was when spending quality time with Cherry.

Mostly, Dexter's father was a fierce politician who never veered from the policies that would further the Harrison family's business and political agenda. The world wouldn't forgive Raymond Harrison for being beholden to that sort of control, even though if humans were truly being honest with themselves, they knew all about it. In truth, "it" was exactly why Dexter had gone along with such deception for so many years and why Amy would rather destroy herself than expose the lies. They were influenced by the strongest drive of all, a parent's love.

"I understand," Dexter finally answered.

"That's good, Dexter. We're going to take the least destructive action. So let's get to it. We don't have much time to stop the bleeding."

CHAPTER 14

DEXTER FRAMPTON

*J*ames offered to give Dexter a ride back to the estate, but he chose to walk instead. It was five miles away. He would normally run six miles on the mornings his schedule allowed the exercise. So a five-mile brisk walk was nothing. A drop of rain fell on the tip of his nose, and he looked up. Dark clouds were gathering above. Soon, the sky would be unleashing water onto the earth. Dexter welcomed the down-pour. Each intake of cold air in his lungs reminded him that there was a lot at stake at the moment.

He needed to feel something besides anger at his parents, Mars, and even Robin for possibly leading him on. He trekked over the stone bridge that straddled Orchard Stream. A memory of

Robin lying beside him—her naked body, soft skin, and wayward strands of hair kissing her face—got him hard. He missed being inside her, kissing her so deep that it felt as if they would catch on fire.

Dexter tossed his head back, squeezed his fist, and shouted, "Fuck!"

He lusted after Robin Hester too damn much and loved her even more.

Then the rain came, and he focused his thoughts on how washed-out Amy looked these days. The truth was, they had more in common than not. As she pursued the sort of man who could never be loyal, who hadn't the capacity or will to love her back, so did he. He never was the marrying type, even though he had gotten married once before. His relationship with his ex-wife, Luddie, could have never worked out. When they'd first met, she had a mental checklist for how a relation-ship should work. He was drawn to the idea of living by a script. Cherry was the least conventional woman he knew. Perhaps if he could do what society said made a person happy, then he would find bliss.

He and Luddie had Maribel and Mariana so fast that his head had spun. Maribel was his oldest, and during Luddie's pregnancy, he'd dreaded the moment of her arrival, feeling as if he were tumbling deeper down the rabbit hole. But on the day he walked into the nursery to have his private time with his daughter, and her bright-green eyes gazed so vulnerably at him, he knew he would spend the rest of his life loving her more than any other person in the world. He loved that feeling. Unlike his father, he would always be there for her. Then one night, between many days of not having sex with Luddie, they did it again, and into the world came Mariana, who Dexter loved just as much as his first daughter. Yes, he loved being their father, but Luddie wanted more children, and for a short time, he allowed her to drag him down every road of trying to conceive another until one day he said, "Stop, no more."

"Okay," she said in a pragmatic tone. "Then we should get a divorce."

She said they wanted different things out of life and had since the day they'd said *I do*. Dexter wanted to continue nurturing a burgeoning career as a screenwriter that had started taking him away from home for months at a time. Luddie wanted all the things that came with a white picket fence. Dexter hadn't known how to desire what Luddie craved so much until he laid eyes on Robin Hester.

The moment he'd sunk his solid erection into her wet, warm, and tight pussy, he'd known he wanted to be inside her and only her until the day he died.

And so, Dexter decided after fighting for his family, he would battle Mars to win her heart. He walked off the main road that led back to the estate because he didn't want to be spotted by security. He was sure they had figured out he was gone by then and had sent a detail out to look for him. The sky had let loose two hours ago, but he wasn't that wet from walking through the forest. He had learned how to navigate the field of trees during the summers he would spend at the orchard with Cherry and Ray. Soon Maggie would arrive, and he suspected the presidential motorcade as well. He made his way to the main road, and since he had on his athletic shoes and pants, he decided he had burned enough time and needed to run the rest of the way.

He hadn't gotten a quarter mile up the road before a silver sedan with dark-tinted windows pulled up alongside him. Dexter stopped running and bent over, clutching his thighs while catching his breath. The window rolled down, and he stretched his neck out farther.

"Dad?" he asked, sounding shocked. "Where

are…" Then he saw two Secret Service men in the back seat.

"Get in, son," Ray said, looking comfortable behind the wheel.

With one look at his father, Dexter's nerves went through the roof. He would have rather continued running, even though he was soaked to his shoes and his toes felt like icicles. He could insist on running, but the president of the United States was telling him to get into the car, and he was sure if he ran another fifteen minutes in the icy rain, he would end up with a cold or worse, pneumonia. So Dexter pulled the door handle and got in.

THE TENSION WAS HIGH, BUT HIS FATHER HADN'T said a word yet. The Secret Service men were on their telecommunication devices, planning their arrival at the gate. It was Ray's second presidential term but the first time Dexter had ever been around Ray living as the most powerful man in the land. It felt strange.

"So how long has it been?" his father asked. "Six years?"

Dexter kept his eyes forward. "About that long."

Ray glanced at him. "Why in the hell were you out running in the rain, son?"

"Had to get you here somehow."

Ray didn't say anything, so Dexter took a quick look at him. His mouth was clenched tightly. Immediately, Dexter wanted to apologize for being the match that had lit the dynamite blowing up his legacy.

"Sorry, Ray," he finally said. "I should've taken Jessica St. James more serious."

The president rubbed his stubbly chin. "It's fine. Cherry told me what happened. I've never asked you to compromise your integrity for me and never will. You did the right thing."

Then why do I feel so wrong? "Thanks, Dad."

As Ray stopped in front of the gate, he turned to Dexter with a genuine smile. "You look good, son."

Dexter smiled back. "Thanks," he said, choosing not to say that he felt like crap. Being emotionally honest was not the sort of relationship he had with his father, a man he hadn't laid eyes on outside of a television screen in six years.

THE PROPERTY WAS BUZZING WITH EXTRA SECURITY. Once he stepped into the foyer, Dexter saw Laurelyn and General Douglas Roth, who was a tall man with an imposing build, sitting in the grand living room, sipping cocktails. When Maggie had insinuated that she would be thorough, she hadn't been exaggerating.

As soon as Dexter stepped inside, he took off his shoes and socks. Cherry walked into sight from the dining area. She and Ray beamed at each other upon first look. Dexter used to love seeing them ogle each other, but now it infuriated him.

Frowning bitterly, he realized someone was missing. "Where's Amy?" he asked his mother.

Cherry rolled her eyes as she shook her head. "Amy's being a brat. She locked herself in her bedroom."

Dexter sighed curtly. The fact that Amy's parents were on the sofa, laughing it up and enjoying a cocktail as though they were having a Sunday garden party pissed him off.

"Oh, Dexter's here," Laurelyn sang as he took off toward Amy's room. He kept going without acknowledging her. There was no way Amy was going to pout her way out of sitting in on what would happen next. The time had come for her to be a fucking adult and fight for her peace of mind like a grown-ass woman.

Down the terra-cotta-paved floor he went, then up two flights of curved steps until he reached the third floor. Amy had been put on the third floor for a reason, to keep her out of the way and out of everyone's hair. Dexter knew for certain, even though Ray had never voiced it to him, that his father would rather Amy not visit the property at all. He always complained about how she flirted with the men who worked in the mill and created a ruckus. As Dexter banged on the door, it occurred to him that his father didn't like Amy at all, nor did they have a real relationship beyond the occasional photo op.

"It's Dexter," he shouted at the top of his lungs.

Suddenly, the music was off, and after a few beats, the door opened. Amy was wearing a plush housecoat, and her eyes and face were red.

"What do you want?" she snapped.

He put his hands on her shoulders and made sure she maintained eye contact with him. "I want you to get your shit together. I want you to speak like a woman who graduated from one of the top private schools in the country. We need you. I need you to be that person when Maggie Adams gets here. Put all your shit on the table with our parents and don't hold back."

"Why the fuck is the big and bad general here?" she asked.

"So you can look him in the eyes and tell him to fuck off. You can tell him and your mother about how fucking selfish they were making you keep their shit a secret. This is it, Amy. This is our chance to fight back, to free ourselves. Get yourself together and get downstairs and fucking face them."

Dexter turned around and stomped away. He would leave it up to her to make the final choice, but that look in her eyes was something between fear, anger, and hope. She would need all of them working on her heart and mind to show up for herself, and he prayed that she would.

DEXTER TOOK A QUICK HOT SHOWER AND CHANGED into a pair of solid-colored dress pants and a cashmere sweater. He couldn't ignore his scratchy throat. *Fuck.* All the other stresses of the last three days had already been working on him, then he'd decided to take a long walk and run in the freezing rain. Regardless, he was ready for whatever was to come out of Maggie's meeting with the family. The fact that the president, first lady, and general had decided to show up was big and truly spoke to the reach of Maggie Adams's power.

One of the maids buzzed Dexter's room on the intercom to tell him dinner was served and the special guest had arrived. Just hearing that brought back his anxiety. His head was dizzy, and all he wanted to do was crawl into bed and sleep.

"Get it together, Dexter," he said to himself then closed his eyes to let the wooziness pass. It was game time.

The guests were already seated in the dining room when he got downstairs. The president sat at one end of the table and the general at the other. On the right side, Dexter sat beside Maggie Adams, who had no food in front of her, and across from them sat Cherry and Laurelyn. Amy's chair was still empty.

The chef had announced that the Michelin-Star-styled glazed bird was Cornish hen with sweet lemon risotto on fresh garden stew. Then the man in the white coat backed out of the dining room. And now they were alone.

"Ms. Adams, how can your service benefit us?" Ray asked.

All eyes were set on the woman who wore a

black turtleneck sweater against her porcelain skin. Dexter had known Ms. Adams for quite a while, and no matter what the setting was, she wore dark colors. He hadn't known her to be a grim kind of person, but she dressed like one.

"There are multiple ways of going about this, but telling the whole truth is off the table, and I'm sure you all agree with me on that," Maggie said.

"I don't," Amy said.

Everyone looked at Amy, who walked into the private dining room and sat in the empty chair.

"You know, I'm sick and tired of being your shame," she said with her glare pinned on General Roth's face.

Her biological father quickly looked down at his plate, but the intense frown on his face and the way he straightened his back and squared his shoulders spoke volumes about how he felt regarding what his daughter had just said.

"You see, this is the fucking problem," Dexter said.

"Dexter, watch your language at the table," Cherry said.

"Mother, I love you, but no. One day she"—he pointed at Amy—"is going to break. And your fucking house of cards will go up in fucking flames.

I've been your good boy, Mom and Dad, but that's over."

"Dexter, let me handle it," Maggie said.

He held up a hand to halt her. "No, Maggie, not until they all see Amy sitting there in front of them and actually give a damn about her. All the shit she's always getting into is about getting your attention, Roth, Laurelyn, and Ray."

"You're the reason we're fucking sitting here, so you shut the hell up," Roth roared.

Dexter snorted as he snarled. "I'm not afraid of you. What kind of father have you been? You made her the fucking mess she is."

"Dexter!" Cherry and Laurelyn said at the same time.

"And Mom, you made me the fucking mess I am."

Cherry shot to her feet and looked wild-eyed at Dexter. "Enough. We heard you. Now shut the hell up and let this young lady finish."

"Did you really hear me, Cherry?"

"Yes. We did, and that's why we're all here. Let's keep moving forward and see where we end up."

Dexter almost believed her, but time would tell. A wave of dizziness rippled through his head as he turned to Maggie and nodded.

Maggie frowned at him then glared at the other faces at the table. "My people have to work fast. We can change the narrative within forty-eighty hours."

Maggie pointed to Cherry. "You fell in love with Ray when you were twenty-two. Your affair was brief, but you remained friends. You never told the president that your son was his. Remember Leonard Knowlton."

Cherry's mouth fell open, then she closed it to swallow. "How did you know about him?" she barely asked.

"Secrets always want to find their way out into the open," Maggie said before turning to Ray. "You know about him, Mr. President?"

Ray's eyes narrowed to slits. Dexter could hardly breathe evenly. He could tell some ugly shit was about to be revealed.

"I know who he is," Ray muttered.

The only time Dexter had seen Ray look so angry was during interviews when he was sparring against his political opponents.

"There's no way you acquired information on Leonard in a matter of hours," Ray said.

"You're right." Maggie nodded. "My agency was hired to perform a deep background check on you six years ago by one of your political opponents. We call the sort of information we found on Leonard Knowlton deep code red. The intelligence discovered had the potential to negatively alter the lives of too many non-political actors. So we kept the intel and buried it."

Dexter punched the table. "Who is Leonard Knowlton?"

"He thought he was your biological father," Cherry said.

Dexter sniffed, laughing cynically. "Another fucking lie. Not surprised. What next?" He wanted to blow his top and throw something. But instead he kept his gaze trained on Maggie's face, pretending as if no one else was at the table. He didn't want to see them right now. He was ready to get the hell out of there and go only God knew where.

"I said 'thought,' Dexter," Cherry said. "Ray is your father."

Maggie watched him with wrinkled brows. Then she took a deep breath. "Right, but Leonard made quite a stink regarding the contrary before he died."

"No," Ray said. "My son is *my* son. My term will be over in three years." He pounded the table. "I want to know my grandchildren, goddamn it. I want to be with the woman I love. Three more years. I've been holding on to three more years."

Laurelyn heaved a sigh. "Do we have to take the fall?" Her gaze begged Maggie for the answer she wanted to hear.

"What did I say, Mr. President?" Maggie asked him.

Ray clenched his lips.

"I told you, the truth will not set you free."

"I want the truth to be told." Amy pointed at the general. "I want that man to admit to the world he's my father."

"No, I will deny it," Roth blurted. "I have a wife and three sons!"

Amy jumped to her feet and angled her body toward him. "And a daughter! You have four fucking kids. Me! I'm your daughter. I'm Douglas Roth's fucking daughter, his secret shame!" Then she started wailing at the top of her lungs and repeating, "Nobody loves me."

Fortunately, Laurelyn beat Dexter to her, as she should have. Laurelyn cradled her daughter in her arms while rocking her, kissing her face, and saying, "I love you."

Seeing Amy's pain made Cherry sniff back tears. Ray was about to get up to console her, but she raised a hand, halting him. Knowing his mother, Dexter knew she didn't want to parade their love in Amy's face. Everyone at the table knew Roth and Laurelyn used to be nothing more than occasional fuck-buddies. And sure, the guy was married, but he wasn't loyal to any woman. He preferred strippers and prostitutes and women he could use and let go. That didn't mean he wasn't a great tactical strategist. The two should've remained mutually exclusive, but in a world of politics rampant with puritanical hypocrisy, they weren't.

Finally, Laurelyn took Amy out of the room. Hardly anyone touched their dinner, and Dexter was sure his mother realized what a bad idea it had been to have a discussion like the one they were having with food.

"You'll be rolling the dice if you tell the truth, Mr. President," Maggie said to Ray.

He opened his mouth to say something.

She raised a hand. "But you might be able to win this one with changes to your polices. People have short memories. You're the villain today and the hero tomorrow. Be the good guy, and they'll be more forgiving."

Laurelyn reentered the room and stood behind the chair she'd abandoned.

"You're going to have to tell the truth about Amy," Maggie said.

Laurelyn stood up straight. "I want nothing more. It's time to end this charade. We're not married. You know that, don't you?"

"I do," Maggie said with a nod.

"Then we tell the truth about my daughter. I won't reveal the name of her father…"

"What are you talking about, Laurelyn?" Roth asked, looking absolutely miserable. He adjusted uncomfortably in his seat. "You saw her. Let's tell the truth and get it over with. I've served three presidents. It's time to retire."

Dexter was glad the guy had had a change of heart. It showed the tin man actually had a heart.

"No," Ray roared. "We'll tell the truth, but you stay on. You'll keep making this country safe for all of our children, including my granddaughters." He pointed at Dexter. "You bring them here. I want to meet them. I want them to know who I am."

Dexter thought about his daughters, and then Rudolph Harrison, his father's father, came to mind. He had never accepted Cherry or Dexter. Then there were his father's siblings and cousins. The Harrisons as a whole were a dastardly clan.

"I don't know about introducing my daughters into your family, Ray."

"This is our family—your mother, you, me, Laurelyn, Amy, and my grandkids. The rest of them can go to hell."

There was a defiance in his father's eyes that appeared to bring Ray to life. There was no way Dexter could say no to that.

He nodded. "You can meet them, and I'll tell them who you are. My ex-wife will be happy to know that you're prepared to stand on the truth, Dad."

Ray cracked a tiny smile, like he'd done earlier when Dexter had referred to him as "Dad" in the car. It wasn't the first time he'd noticed that Ray preferred Dexter to call him that, but it was definitely one of the few remarkable times the man had securely earned the title.

AMY EVENTUALLY RETURNED BUT ONLY AFTER Maggie had excused herself and ensured the president that the mission to change the narrative had already begun. He would have to direct his White

House staff according to her people's orders until further notice.

"If we're going to have success, then we should see signs of it within eight weeks," she said before leaving.

The rest of dinner was a quiet affair. Anxiety was in the air, and it felt as though Dexter wasn't the only one who couldn't wait to leave the room. Not only was he emotionally drained, but he could hardly keep his eyes open. He also had chills, a burning sensation in the back of his throat, and a headache that could halt a bull. After taking a stab at finishing his dinner, Dexter wiped his mouth, turned to his mother, and said he was finished.

She reached out across the table, and her opened hand asked for his. After a brief hesitation, he gave it to her. Dexter waited for her to say something, but instead she pressed her lips together in an appreciative smile.

"Love you, Mom," he said.

"I love you more."

He winked at her. In a different world, he would test her proclamation. The fact that he'd kept her secrets for so many years at his expense proved who loved whom more. Regardless, he journeyed upstairs.

It would've been the perfect time to call Robin and ask about her dealings with Mars, but he didn't have the energy. He would rest first and contact Robin later.

When Dexter made it to his room, he stripped out of his pants, T-shirt, and dress shirt then crawled under his blankets. It took a while before his aches and pangs would let him drift off to sleep, but eventually he did.

CHAPTER 15

*R*obin folded her arms to control her fidgeting as Claudia and Peter Cantor viewed her installation project. All she could think about was what Theresa had told her regarding the rumors about her and Mars. He had set her up. *What an asshole.* Robin became more nervous because Claudia and Peter were taking too long.

"Wow. I didn't expect this," Peter said, viewing the glowing fragments with wide eyes. "How is this even possible?"

Robin checked the time on her cell phone. If she left soon enough, she could book a flight to Harrison Town, Vermont and get there before sundown.

"Robin?" Claudia asked.

She looked up quickly. "Yeah?"

"Peter asked you a question."

She shook her head tersely, frowning. "What question?"

"How were you able to get the metal to glow with more intensity than the lights?"

"Redirecting," she muttered, keeping her eyes on the screen.

"Yes, but how?" he asked.

She tapped on her messages and saw all the ones from Theresa and Elaine about her involvement with Mars and Dexter. Her mouth fell open as she read the first gossip-rag story.

"Robin?" Claudia scolded.

"What?" she asked sharply.

"Peter asked you a question."

She threw up the hand that wasn't holding her cell phone. "Yes. I heard him. He's here to view all of this. But if he wants to know how I did this, then he can figure it out himself." New messages from friends in different parts of the world kept filtering into her phone.

"I apologize, Peter," Claudia said in her fake accent.

"No, no, no," he said. "Robin's right. If I were

the artist, I wouldn't tell anyone how I did this either."

When Robin looked up, Claudia was smiling pensively.

"Listen, is that it? Because I have a lot to do," Robin said.

"What is happening on your phone that is more important than what we're doing here?"

Robin wanted to advise Claudia to remember to limit her contractions when she was faking a European accent. Contractions were generally an American thing. But she took a breath. Lashing out was something she was capable of when she was emotionally distressed.

"I'm sure it's because of the rumors," Peter said. There was a gleam in his eyes that made him seem as though he were enjoying every aspect of the gossip about her.

"Rumors? What rumors?" Claudia asked.

That was it. It was time for them to leave, and her too. "Maybe Peter can fill you in on your way out."

Claudia fanned her hands out. "No way."

Take another breath, Robin. "Claudia, we're going to have to work together, even in this moment, if you want this installation project to make it to his venue. It'll be my last, you know. That's going to give my showing a lot of value to all your other artists whose work you'll have displayed when my fans walk out of my exhibit."

Claudia laughed delightfully, clearly trying to keep her anger under wraps in front of Peter. "I understand you're under a lot of pressure."

"I said this will be my last showing ever. My last project ever. I'm done with art, and I can do that because I saved a lot of money over the years. However, I will have this final showing, not for me but for you and your other artists, who may be able to benefit from what I've done here."

"Whoa," Peter said. "You're really leaving the scene?"

"Yes, I really am."

He tried to conceal the eagerness on his face as he turned to Claudia then pressed his hands together with controlled restraint. "Then yes, absolutely, Claudia. We will allow our venue to be the landing place for Robin Hester's final showing."

She and Claudia continued staring at each other.

The small Adam's apple in Claudia's throat bobbed up and down as she swallowed. "Are you serious?" she whispered.

"Yes," Robin said an octave too high.

"While you're at the top?"

She nodded softly.

Their soft gazes continued focusing on each other.

"I really thank you for bringing me to that point in my career that I would never let myself land," Robin said somberly. "I'm at the top, and it's not where I want to be."

"Then where do you want to be, Robin?"

She shrugged. "In the long run, I don't know. Right now, I want to be with Dexter."

"Then we should book the date," Peter said.

"No." Claudia raised a finger in objection. "We go back to the Temperance Gallery for your final show."

"Wait a minute," Peter objected.

"No," Robin said. "We have to stay in Brooklyn. That's what I promised the fans who were in the studio during our recording at Lunch Time New York."

"Promises?" Claudia asked. "Who cares about promises, Robin? This is your final show. People will be coming from all over the world to see it."

"I care about the promises I make."

Peter's face lit up. "Then how about the Thursday after next?"

"No," Robin and Claudia said at the same time.

"I'll get back to the both of you with a date later," Robin said.

"What do you mean by later?" Claudia asked.

Peter jerked his head back and eyed Claudia suspiciously. "What did you say?"

Her eyes expanded, probably because she realized she'd lost her accent.

"Listen, both of you," Robin said to cover for Claudia's goof. "This is happening. My fans are going to see this, but first, I have something more important to do."

CLAUDIA AND PETER AGREED TO WAIT TO HEAR from her in the next couple of days or so. Robin had no idea if she would be able to get in touch with Dexter. The Harrison Family Orchard Estate probably had tight security on every inch of the property. He was probably so pissed at her that he didn't want to hear her voice or see her face ever again. He had given her his heart and his trust, and in just one toxic encounter, Mars had destroyed his confidence in her.

What an asshole her ex was. The kisses, sitting too close, controlling his maniacal temper when she questioned him about his relationship with Plume—it was all an act. After all, he was an award-winning actor. She was embarrassed that she'd ever felt anything for the guy, especially lust. These days, Robin wouldn't let him touch her with a ten-foot pole.

As soon as her guests left, she booked a flight online and packed a bag. The Uber driver arrived a half hour later and had plenty of time to get her to the airport. She would be flying out of LaGuardia. On the way over, she read as many stories about Dexter's family as she could. Tomorrow at noon, the president was holding a press conference to confirm that he had a relationship when he was twenty-two years old and had a son. It sounded as though they would not be disclosing that Harrison and Cherry Frampton were married. There was an exposé in the *Times* about how successful Dexter Frampton was and quotes from him about knowing his father growing up and how the Harrisons had had a problem with his mother's background and pedigree. Harrison had been a young man trying to please his father, and everyone could understand that, even him. There was something about what was written that didn't sound like Dexter at all. Robin couldn't put her finger on it, but she was positive he'd never said any of it.

The driver announced they were fifteen minutes away and said they were late because of the pockets of traffic. Robin had been so engrossed in the articles she was reading that she hadn't noticed.

"No problem. I'm early," she said without taking her eyes off a story written about her. This one called her an artist with A-list clientele and accused her of breaking up Mars and Plume Ashbury's engagement. She laughed bitterly at that. That was why she never believed the tabloids. The next story she read cited her latest failed installation project and claimed that their sources said she was hot and heavy with the president's illegitimate son. The same article said that Amy Harrison was not the president's daughter and that her father was a guy named General Douglas Roth.

"What the hell?" Robin muttered. It was like a big Washington, D.C. orgy fest.

Actually, she wasn't that shocked. They were all the types who had public faces that set the standard of what society deemed as decent and aspirational, but they were totally the opposite in private, which indeed made them human.

The car stopped, and when she looked up, she saw they were at arrivals. That was fast. She tipped the driver and headed into the terminal to catch her flight. Since she had no bag to check in, she passed through security and went straight to the gate. Robin occupied herself with more news about the Harrisons and herself. Then her phone rang in her hands. A sense of excitement flooded her when she saw who it was.

She tapped the answer button. "Gran?"

"Hello, darling." Her grandmother sounded very formal.

"You heard," Robin replied, knowing that was the reason for her gran's tone.

"Yes. I have. I didn't know you were involved with the actor. Now I've met Dexter Frampton, of course, and he's a lovely man."

It was as if the words gushed out of Robin's mouth. There wasn't much time before her flight boarded, and she explained as much as she could about how she'd fallen in love with Dexter.

"And yes, Mars was my ex-boyfriend, and being with him was me operating with bad judgment."

"Darling, we're not shaming ourselves today. We

all make mistakes then learn from them. There's no disgrace in that."

Robin smiled. "Thanks, Gran."

Gran fell silent for a moment, but Robin could hear her grandmother smile all the way on the other side of the country.

"Well, what I've read this morning, and what's being reported about the Harrisons and now our family…"

"Our family?"

"It doesn't take the bloodhounds long to sniff out more blood."

Robin hadn't gotten to the stories about the Hesters. Of course, they would figure out she was the granddaughter of the multibillionaire self-made real-estate developer Lorraine Hester.

"I'm so sorry, Grandmother. I should've given you a heads-up."

"It's fine. It's not why I'm calling. Also, it's not why I'm taking your temperature."

"Taking my temperature?"

"Trying to figure out if you can handle another separate, difficult situation."

Robin uncrossed her legs and sat up straight. "I can." No, she couldn't.

Gran paused for a few beats then sighed. "Darling, your mother passed. It happened three months ago."

Without acknowledging the statement until after the moment was over, Robin rose to her feet. "I'm sorry, what did you just say?"

"Your mother. She died three months ago of a heart attack. It was caused by a drug overdose," Gran said with the sort of composure expected of her.

If it weren't Gran on the other line, Robin would've said she had to go and ended the call.

"Darling, are you still there?"

Her throat was so tight that she could barely speak. "Yes."

"The body has been cremated, but dental records, photos, and organ samples confirm that the deceased was your mother."

Your mother. Those two words kept ringing through Robin's head as boarding was announced for her flight.

"Gran, I'm on my way to Vermont to see Dexter. I have to go."

"You're my strongest granddaughter, so I know you'll be fine for now, but when the heartbreak finally hits, promise me you'll call me."

Robin closed her eyes to picture her grand-mother's face. "Gran?"

"Yes, my love?"

"By the way, how are you handling this news?"

"Don't worry about me, darling. I've led your mother to crystal-clear water a million times, but she chose to go back and drink mud. So I've always done the best I could for her. I'm fine."

Robin wiped the tears from under her eyes. She'd had no idea they were rolling. "I love you."

"I love you too," Gran said.

And on that note, without another word, they ended their call.

Once again, Robin appreciated how nosy people were not in New York City. No one even paid attention to her crying. She swiped her bag from beside her feet and went to board her flight.

CHAPTER 16

*A*s the airplane soared through the air, the confusing tears that flooded her eyes before takeoff did not make a recurring appearance. They couldn't. Robin closed her eyes and thought about all the memories she had of Lily Rose, a woman who'd never lived up to her beautiful name. When Robin was a little girl, too young to remember how old she was exactly, she remembered watching her mother on the phone, crying and yelling at a man, accusing him of not loving her and promising him she would leave everything behind to be with him. Robin recalled her little girl's brain wondering, "What about me, Mommy?"

Not too long after that phone call, her mother had disappeared from her life for a little while. She remembered during the days Lily Rose was away, Gran would sing songs to her. One of her favorites was "The Girl With The Gold Paint Brushes."

The tears were back. She wiped them.

That song was the reason she'd asked her gran for paint and brushes as gifts for her next birthday. She may have been seven or eight. Gran had happily given her the gift she'd asked for, but she'd gotten an unexpected present too, one she hadn't wanted. Lily Rose had come back with two black eyes and a busted lip and a comedown from a severe high.

Despite being a drug addict, when her mother wasn't on a binge, she'd known how to at least hire someone to pay the bills, buy the groceries, and get Robin and Theresa off to school. So it was on Robin's birthday that Lily Rose had convinced Gran to give her and Theresa back to their mother. She might as well have been absent. It wasn't until Robin was well into her teens that Lily Rose had found a mean old guy to run off with, and that was the last time Robin had chosen to see her mother.

Robin hated Lily Rose. She wasn't crying because she loved her mother or would miss her. Perhaps she was crying because the announcement of her death ended an era. Her mother being gone abolished the hope that must've lived inside of her, several layers beneath the surface, a hope that one day Lily Rose would be normal. Perhaps it was merely a fantasy.

Yes… That was why Robin was crying. Her fantasy had finally disintegrated into what it was actually worth—nothing.

The tears were rolling so fast that she could hardly keep up. The woman next to her waved at the flight attendant and asked for some tissues. Once she received them, she silently handed them to Robin.

"Thank you," Robin said.

The woman smiled and continued reading her book.

Hell, she loved how New Yorkers could mind their business. Perhaps she should move to Brooklyn. There was no need to go back to LA. And why should she retire her career? There was no need to do that either.

Robin blew her nose again. Then she smiled, slowly and genuinely. She had thought leaving art behind would make her truly feel free, but it wouldn't. What did was learning that Lily Rose had lived her life to the very end. She had done it her way, forsaking her daughters and mother, and loving only herself. Those words of wisdom Sonja had spoken to Robin after Mars had broken her heart rang truer now than ever. As long as there was breath in her body, she would never live or die like Lily Rose—*never*.

Less than two hours later her flight landed, and she disembarked the airplane. It was cold in the terminal. From the big windows, she could see fresh snow layering the earth. Like any native Californian, Robin's long black wool trench coat, ripped jeans, and black leather ankle boots hadn't prepared her for the sort of icy weather that cut right through her skull and froze her brain.

Robin kicked herself for not thinking the weather through. The ticket agent at the counter informed her that she'd gotten as far as she could to Harrison by flight. Then she studied Robin curiously.

"Wait, are you Robin Hester?" the agent asked.

"Who?" Robin asked, thinking fast on her feet.

"The artist. The one who's involved with the illegitimate son?"

"I'm sorry. Illegitimate son?" She couldn't believe this woman was referring to Dexter in that way. People were fucking sheep. That was what Raymond Harrison's political opponents were calling Dexter. The tag sounded so beneath the beautiful, smart, sexy, powerful, and unique man that Dexter Frampton was.

"Yes, the gorgeous guy with the blue eyes," she said as though just thinking about Dexter made her swoon.

"Oh, that story," she said. "I wouldn't call him the illegitimate son, though. I would say he's the president's only son."

The woman leaned closer to Robin. "Oh my God, you are her." She kept her voice low.

Robin's mouth opened then closed as she wondered if it were too late to lie again.

"Do not go to the bus station," the woman whispered. "We have a rule against loitering in this airport, but they've been tipped off by someone at LaGuardia. They know you're on your way."

Robin swallowed a lump in her throat. "When you say they, who are you referring to?"

"Reporters."

The last thing Robin wanted to do was run into reporters and cameras who were looking for a salacious story.

"Listen, I'm off in five minutes. Harrison is two hours away, and I live an hour away. I can get you to my town. I have a friend who works at the local car rental company. She will get you a car, keep your name off the record, and you can drive the rest of the way to Harrison."

"You would do that for me?" Robin asked, so thankful that the woman had offered.

"Yes, I would, but I also should confess that I was in New York City in August, and I was lucky enough to see Soulscape Part One."

"You did?" Robin barely asked.

"Yes, I did. And I heard the Berlin showing of Soulscape Part Two wasn't as successful but that you've revised it and are showing again in Brooklyn."

"Damn. Good news travels fast," Robin said.

"I received an alert on my phone two hours ago," the attendant said.

"You want tickets, right?"

The attendant looked at her dubiously. "No. I want to know if it's really going to be your last show. The DM said your showing in Brooklyn will be your last."

Robin groaned as she rolled her eyes, remembering that she should probably text Claudia and tell her that she'd changed her mind.

"No." Robin shook her head. "I changed my mind."

"And that's a girl's prerogative," the gate attendant said. Then she told Robin to go with her so that they could leave out of one of the employee exits.

Surprisingly, the gate attendant's name was Robin as well—Robyn with a Y and not an I. Her last name was Hargrave, and they both thought it was cool that their surnames began with an H. The car ride seemed to fly by as their conversation flowed with Robyn Hargrave talking about her two daughters and ex-husband.

"I swear I hate leaving my babies every day to drive an hour away from home to work."

She told Robin that she would've driven her all the way to Harrison but that she only had a limited number of hours to spend with her girls before they went to bed, and she didn't want to waste any of them.

"I understand." Robin truly did. If she had kids, she would want to be near them all the time too.

While Dexter was hiding out with Robin, not a day had gone by in which he didn't want to call his daughters. He'd actually had his assistant carry messages to them. They would send word back to him, and everything they'd said had made his face light up like the sun.

Robin was able to confide in Robyn about just learning of her mother's death and how indifferent she was about it and why. Robyn shared how abusive her ex-husband was.

"I picked him because I used to see my own mom get the shit kicked out of her by my dad. He did it so much that he ended up killing her. Now he's serving life in prison without the possibility of parole."

"Wow," Robin said.

"My mother was weak, like your mother. She couldn't leave my father because she was addicted to him. In prison for life, and my dad is still a mean-ass, selfish prick. May he rot behind bars first and in hell next."

It fell silent as Robin wondered what she wished for her mother.

"A do-over," she said. "May God grant my mother a do-over to redeem herself."

Robyn grunted thoughtfully. "I like the idea of do-overs. I wouldn't want one, but I'm sure my mom could use one of those too."

Robin and Robyn smiled at each other and talked about Robyn's plan to find a job closer to home so that she could take some online courses. She'd always wanted to be a pediatrician, and so what that she was twenty-five and probably would be thirty before she had her ducks in a row. Come hell or high water, one day she would be a doctor.

"I might be fifty before I graduate from med school, though. I have to put my girls through college at some point."

They pulled into the parking lot of the rental-car place. Robyn turned off the engine and leaned forward to look up at the sky through her windshield. "Hallelujah, we beat the snow. But we better hurry up and get you in and out so you don't have to fight it. Have you ever driven in the snow?"

Robin couldn't stop smiling at her new friend. It was just ironic on a day like today that she would meet someone so genuine who felt like a friend Robin had known forever.

"Never," Robin replied.

Robyn opened door. "Then let's go before it gets worse!"

"Robyn?"

The young woman turned to look at her. "What is it?"

"I just wanted to say thank you."

Robyn pressed a hand over her heart. "Ah… You're welcome."

"And also, I believe you're going to get everything your heart desires. I truly do."

Robyn smiled. "Well, from your mouth to God's ears."

With that said, Robin got out of the car. It took less than five minutes for Robyn's friend Phoebe to put Robin in a car and send her on her way. They both wanted the Californian to get on the road before she ended up having to drive in heavy snowfall. And to help preserve her anonymity, the car was put in Phoebe's name. The plan was that Robin would have dinner at Robyn's house, with or without Dexter, before catching a flight back to New York.

Robyn and Phoebe were so right about driving in the snow. It happened all of a sudden and was coming down hard. At least she was driving a four-wheel-drive SUV. The vehicle was sturdy enough to make her feel safe. Visibility was low, and to make matters worse, she had to use back roads. According to Phoebe, most of the roads leading to Harrison were closed because the president was in town. But only a few people knew about Crestline Highway. The route couldn't be found on any map, so Phoebe wrote down the instructions on how to find it. So not only did Robin have to navigate slippery roads with nightfall closing in on her, she had to read words on a page too. But surprisingly, once she was on Crestline, the rest of the route was one straight line, leading to Harrison Family Orchard Estate. According to the navigational map on her dashboard, she was less than a mile away.

Until that very moment, she hadn't tried to figure out what she should say to Dexter. *Keep it simple, stupid,* she reminded herself.

I love you, and I would never choose Mars over you. That kiss was manipulated by Mars. I never saw it coming. Sure, I should've kept my distance. I wanted to. But when I saw him, I wasn't thinking clearly. Not because I was so flustered by my longing for him. I have no longing for him…

Robin moaned painfully as she sighed. Maybe she shouldn't think about it so hard.

Suddenly, the light in the guard station was visible. It was showtime. Steadying her breaths became laborious as she stopped right in front of the tall black iron gates, which had a family crest engraved in the center. Two guards came out of the shed. One walked to the passenger's side window and the other stood at the driver's side. Robin conjured her most friendly smile before rolling down the window.

"How can I help you, ma'am?"

The guy was very young and had a small red pimple on his left cheek. Robin could remember distinguishing marks like that whenever she was nervous.

"I'm here to see Dexter Frampton."

"Good try, but you need to turn around and drive back to wherever you came from."

Goodness, he sounded and looked so cold. His boyish features and soft muddy-blue eyes convinced her the hard-nosed stance he was taking did not reflect the real person inside.

"Excuse me, sir, but I'm his girlfriend, Robin Hester."

The young guard studied her with eyes narrowed to slits. She could see he was unsure about what to do next. "Give me a second," he said.

He conferred with the other guard at the back of the truck, so she couldn't see them. Soon, he was back.

"Listen, ma'am, we were given strict instructions to not let anyone in while the first lady's here. You should come back tomorrow."

"But I came a long way to see him. I promise he'll want to talk to me."

"It's not up to him, ma'am. He's the reason why security's as tight as it is in the first place."

Her frown intensified. "Sorry?"

"Ma'am, you have to go. I would let you in if it were up to me, but it's not." Finally, his eyes softened, and he showed his real self behind the strong front-gate-guard persona. For a second, she wondered how often others saw the real him.

The trees at the edge of the gate caught Robin's attention. She remembered Dexter telling her stories about how he would sneak off the compound during lockdown, which occurred whenever Cherry and Ray were there together. The only way Dexter could bring his friends onto the property to swim in some of the best natural swimming ponds the state had to offer was to sneak them on.

Even though it was snowing, Robin was not going to drive into town and find somewhere to lodge for the night. Heck, she didn't have the patience for that. She'd come there with a mission —to see Dexter. He needed to know how much she wanted to be with him. She needed him to hold her, kiss her forehead, and tell her he loved her and would never hurt her.

"All right. Thank you," she briskly said to the guard.

He apologized again and stood between her and the gate as she backed up the car, turned around, and went the opposite direction. The snowfall had lightened up a bit. As she drove up the road, she made sure she was out of the guards' sight before making a turn down one of the roads she'd spotted earlier. Finally, she saw her opportunity to make a left and took it.

Robin realized she was in an environment that was foreign to her. She'd gone camping a number of times and had a lot of respect for nature. It held all the power. Trekking through the snow in the forest was not her ideal circumstance, but she was hyped on adrenaline. Something else was happening inside her too, and she was sure it had something to do with Lily Rose's death.

A blanket of sadness covered her, but it was not the time to cry. She had to think. Robin slowed her speed and looked for any trail that would allow her the opportunity to make a right. The sky was purple. Soon it would be totally dark, so she had to find a pathway heading back toward the compound soon.

She was rolling along at three miles per hour, checking the navigational map on the dashboard and the tree line for a viewable right turn. So far, she'd seen nothing. Robin thought perhaps she should forget it. Only she couldn't. Then, as the headlights illuminated the gravelly roadside, she saw the turn she had been hoping existed. Robin sped up to take it.

The road wasn't paved with cement but was layered with a couple of inches of snow instead. The ride was bumpy, the way narrow, and definitely not made for a vehicle as large as the one she was driving. It was darker among the trees. Robin was beginning to question her judgment. She was more rational than how she was behaving. One side of her brain was telling her to stop the SUV, put it in reverse, and carefully back up until her wheels hit cement and ice. But she didn't listen to that side of her brain; she obeyed the other.

According to the map on her dash, she was closer to the compound than she had been before turning off the road. Plus, she didn't want to get too close because common sense told her security was swarming the surrounding woods, making sure others didn't do exactly what she was doing. So Robin decided it was a good time to stop and walk the rest of the way.

Since it was cold enough to freeze her nipples off, she dug into her backpack and put on another sweater and two more pairs of socks. She debated between wearing athletic shoes, which would help her feet get her there quicker, or putting on her leather ankle boots with the smaller heel. If she recalled correctly, leather didn't always mean warmer. Plus, her athletic shoes had an extra layer of padding, so she put them on.

Robin collected her purse and grabbed her bag. It wasn't that heavy, and she wasn't going that far. As soon as she stepped out of the vehicle, the cold mugged her. Her ears froze, and so did her fingers.

"Hell," she muttered.

She walked to the rear of the vehicle and shined her cell phone light up the path toward the road. Her instincts were confirmed. She had to veer off the path and toward the south. Robin stood very still, allowing her eyes to adjust to the dark. Snowflakes peppered her face. And damn, was it cold. But she knew all she had to do was make it to the front door, knock, then Dexter would know she had shown up to fight for their love.

ROBIN HAD BEEN WALKING IN THE SNOW FOR AT least an hour. She couldn't feel her fingers or toes anymore. Her lips were numb. Unfortunately she couldn't look up at the sky and let the moon tell her if she was still heading south.

She heard a crack then felt the cold water cover her foot all the way to her calf. "Shit," she yelled as loudly as she could, knowing there was no one around to hear her. Never had she felt so lonely.

It was time to accept that it had been a bad idea to start on her journey while it was not only turning dark but snowing. She couldn't retrace her steps back to the car. She had to keep moving forward, hoping she would run into the gates of the property or someone on the security detail.

As her eyelids weighed heavily and her feet felt as though they had turned to ice, Robin knew she had to do a better job of thinking than she had been doing. She couldn't even feel her cell phone between her fingers as she took it out of her pocket. Thank goodness she had one bar, which allowed her at least one phone call. She struggled to make it, and thank God, she got through.

CHAPTER 17

DEXTER FRAMPTON

33 Minutes Ago

The night Dexter and his family experienced life-changing moments at the dinner table, he was so wiped out that he went straight to bed. In the morning, Carlotta, one of the house attendants, knocked on his door to wake him up for breakfast. When he heard his name being called, all he could do was moan. His head ached, and his throat was on fire. Even with the heavy blanket over him, he couldn't get warm enough. Even though he felt like shit, all he wanted was to be left alone so that he could sleep some more.

Then he felt the back of a hand against his forehead. Carlotta said something about hot tea with healing herbs. He went back to sleep. At some point, she was insisting he finish drinking a lukewarm beverage that had some sweetness and heat to it.

Dexter woke up, and his bladder was full. After rushing to the attached bathroom to relieve himself, he went back into his room and stood at the window. It was getting dark and snowing. He pieced together the last moments he was conscious, recalling how he felt as if he were about to die. But now the only part of his body that felt aches and pangs was his heart. One face filled his thoughts. Dexter jumped into a pair of pajamas and hurried to his office. He swiped his cell phone off his desk and turned it on.

"Shit!" he shouted. It was still out of service.

He needed to know how long he'd been out of commission. His eyes found the time and date on an electronic clock, which was nailed to the wall. Holy shit, he'd been asleep for the better part of two days.

"There you are!" Cherry sang.

"Mom." He held up his device. "No phone service still? Why not?"

She smashed her hands on her waist. "Well, I'm glad you're better." Her tone indicated that she felt there were more important things for Dexter to focus on than his phone.

Right away, he knew to adjust his attitude. "I apologize for my tone. Yes, I have to thank Carlotta for whatever she gave me. But with all due respect, either I get phone service, or I'm getting the hell off this compound."

Cherry sighed tiredly. "I knew what you were coming in here, looking for."

He looked down at her hand. She was holding a cell phone and handed it to him.

"Does it work?"

"It has limited ability. You can call Vincent Adams at least and keep your mind occupied with your work."

"Mom, it's not enough."

"It's almost over, Dexter. We're at the tail end of this."

Dexter rubbed the inner corners of his eyes. He so desperately wanted to get back to Robin to find out what the hell was behind the kiss she'd had with Mars.

"You have forever to be in love. We're just

asking for, at the most, twenty-four more hours. I'm leaving shortly. Tomorrow, I'll be interviewed by BCN after your father's press conference."

"I still don't understand why I have to be here."

"Because as soon as you leave here, you'll be accosted by reporters."

"You know I won't say anything."

"I know." Her eyes softened even more. "But please, son. Twenty-four hours, then we'll have the driver take you to the airfield, and you'll fly on the private airplane home."

"I don't need that, Mom. I'd rather fly commercial."

She brushed the side of his face. "I know, sweetheart. You always liked going back to normal after your father was around. Is that why you haven't seen him in six years?"

Dexter pursed his lips. Apparently, his parents had been pillow-talking again. "The list of reasons is too long, but I'll stay." He wiggled the phone in his hand. "I want to call Vince."

She seemed torn. Knowing Cherry, she wanted to hear that list. Suddenly, the phone rang, and he answered it without pause.

"Hello?"

"Dexter?" It wasn't Vince.

"Sonja?"

"Robin is out there somewhere in the cold and the dark. I lost contact with her. You have to go find her."

He was frowning so hard that his vision blurred. "Robin is where?"

"She went to see you. They wouldn't let her in the gate, so she tried walking in the wilderness. She took a path off… Oh my God… I can't remember the road. She said it was the first right after leaving your compound and then the first right into the woods. It's dark. She's cold, and I don't know if she's going to make it."

"Calm down, Sonja. We're going to find her. I'll get back to you when she's safe." He ended the call. "Mom, I'm going to have to get the hell off this compound, and I'm going to need all security searching the woods."

He was walking so fast that he could hear feet running behind him, trying to keep up.

"Who's out in the woods?" Cherry asked.

"Robin."

"Oh no. It's dark and snowing. What's she doing in the woods?"

There was no use chastising his mother for ordering the guards at the gate to be strict. They could've at least called the house and asked for him. However, Dexter knew Cherry would've told them to send Robin away, and his beautiful, sexy, smart, and oh-so-sensual girlfriend—yes, girlfriend—would've done exactly what she'd done and ended up lost in the woods in the freezing cold.

Shit, she came to see me…

"Mom, I'm taking your Hummer. Call the guards and tell them to open the gates, or I'm going to bust right through them." When he made it down the stairs, he turned and faced Cherry. "I need the keys."

At first, she hesitated. It wasn't like Cherry to let such a moment go to waste. He needed something from her, and she wanted more information from him.

"Mom, keys," he insisted.

He followed her to the small table near the large windows. She opened the top drawer, took a set of keys out, and put them in his hand. "Be safe. Find her."

Dexter ran back upstairs, dressed in the warmest gear he had, and headed out.

Dexter had no problem getting past the gates. He remembered what Sonja had said about the route Robin had taken and followed it to a T. He found her SUV sitting in the dark and parked behind it.

He knew that part of the woods. It was the hardest to navigate. Dexter's first plan was to track her footsteps. Even though her steps were snowed over, not enough had fallen to cover them completely. So he pointed the high-powered flashlight at the snow until he found where she had taken her first steps and let traces of Robin lead him to her.

Dexter kept his anxiety under control. He had to work meticulously. He could see where she could've gotten lost. All the usual trails back to the estate were covered with snow. If she'd missed one, she would have gone off in a different direction. He came to a familiar part, and his instincts told him that was exactly what had happened.

"Robin!" he shouted once again. His voice echoed. Someone else called her name too, but they were too far south to actually find her.

Dexter wanted to bolt forward, but he had to

remain vigilant, following what looked most like her tracks in the snow.

"Robin!" he called over and over.

And that was when he heard her shout. "I'm here!"

CHAPTER 18

She had heard once that when a person was freezing to death, the warmest place to be was near the earth, curled up in a ball. So when she couldn't progress an inch farther, Robin found a spot by a tree, under which there was no snow, and lay there in a fetal position.

She'd gotten ahold of Sonja and had given her pretty good directions to where help could find the vehicle she'd abandoned. Robin didn't know how much will to live she had left in her. Tolerating the cold had been pure agony.

Suddenly, she was swept up into strong arms. She didn't know whether she were dead or alive. Only seconds ago, a man who sounded like Dexter had called her name, and she had kept repeating,

"Here." Was she still saying it? His body was so warm. He was moving so fast.

She struggled to keep her eyelids lifted as she heard a door open and she was put into the back seat of a large vehicle.

"Baby, stay with me!"

It was him. "Dexter?" she whispered.

"It's me. I'm going to turn some heat on. Can you stay awake?"

"Mm-hmm."

It was warming up. He took her wet shoes and socks off. Her coat, pants, and shirt came off next. Then he wrapped a thick blanket around her.

"Better?" he asked.

"Mm-hmm," she said again.

He squeezed her toes. "Can you feel this?"

"I can."

"That's good, baby."

"I missed you," she managed to say.

"I missed you too." His lips were on hers, and she kissed him back. "I want you to lie here and get warm. The heat is on full blast. I'm going to go out and handle some things."

The more comfortable she felt, the more she was able to open her eyes. That was when she noticed the flashing lights. Dexter kissed her one more time before heading out into the freezing cold.

She heard men's voices, then another man opened the door and asked her a lot of questions about how her limbs felt.

"I'm going to examine your feet, okay?" he asked.

"Okay," she muttered. He poked her with something sharp, and she flinched. "Ouch."

"That's good, real good."

He did the same with her fingers, and she had the same reaction. "All right, then, you're good," the man said. Then the door slammed shut.

A lot was happening. Dexter got back in the vehicle and started backing up. "You can rest now, babe."

"I can?" she whispered.

"Yes. I'm taking you to the house."

Robin was so tired, comfortable, and warm now that she was out of the cold and wrapped in the blanket. She let herself drift off into a light sleep. When they got back to the estate, Dexter swept her in his arms and carried her into the house and upstairs. He tucked her into his big, comfortable, and more importantly, oh-so-warm bed. She went to sleep immediately and didn't wake up until a long time after when she felt something soft and dreamy beneath her and something hard and virile around her. The light in the room was dim. The erotic feeling of warmth was inescapable.

"Are you awake?" Dexter asked in a voice laced with concern and yearning.

She groaned at how woozy she still felt. "I'm still tired, but I'm nice and cozy, especially since you're right here with me."

"Mmm," he said as though he liked the sound of that. Then he grinded his virile erection between her ass cheeks.

Robin sighed as her pussy tingled with a voracious need.

Dexter guided himself on top of her, spreading her legs as he thrust his throbbing manhood inside her. Robin opened her eyes wide and gasped as he filled her. His mumbles told her how wet, warm, and tight her pussy was gripping his dick. Passion ran amuck. Her heart was bursting. Tears flowed. He kissed them then her lips.

"I love you, Robin Hester," he whispered in her ear as he plunged deep inside her.

The back of her head pressed against the pillow as she let out a deep sigh. "I love you too, Dexter Frampton."

"Shit," he uttered then rapidly shifted in and out of her.

Withstanding the pleasurable sensations made her clench her teeth. Oh, goodness gracious, she loved how quickly Dexter brought her to climax when he did that. And her pussy was sensitive, alive, and yearning for the final sensation.

"Oh, damn, baby… I'm coming," he said breathlessly.

She knew to help him out when he said that. She adjusted her hips and guided the spot where her orgasm was sparking toward his dick.

"Ah!" she cried as he stimulated her more and more. Then Robin screamed when it happened.

And that was when Dexter whimpered and quaked as he exploded inside her.

THE ENDORPHINS OF AFTER-SEX MADE THEM chuckle. Robin was on cloud nine as Dexter carefully flipped her on top of him, keeping his softening manhood in her soaking-wet pussy. He moaned at her deliciousness as he plunged himself deeper inside her.

"That kiss between Mars and I was not real," she said, feeling relieved to get those words off her chest. "He showed up at the restaurant where I was having lunch with Claudia. She went outside to take a call, then he came in, and the first thing he did was kiss me."

"Then it wasn't real?"

Robin looked him in the eyes. "Hell no." Then she closed her eyes and sighed gravely. "But my gran called me to tell me that my mom died."

"I know. Sonja told me when I called her last night after bringing you in out of the cold."

"She knows I'm safe, then?"

"Yes, she does. She's on her way here, along with your sister and grandmother. I invited them. Do you mind?"

Her smile must've shown how bright she felt on the inside. "No, I don't mind," she said excitedly.

"My daughters and their mother will be arriving as well. My father, the president, also." He tilted his head cautiously. "How does that make you feel?"

She raised her eyebrows. "Nervous but excited."

He smiled. "Me too." Then he frowned. "Last night, I was scared as hell. What made you go into the woods like that?"

Robin felt the corners of her mouth turn down. Then she shook her head. "I wasn't thinking it through. I just wanted to see you. It's like, I wasted so many months staying away from you because I was afraid of how being near you made me feel. And now I'm embracing that feeling, and it's like… euphoric. When you stopped calling me, I thought the longer I waited to explain my side of the rumors, the more you wouldn't love me the same."

He kissed the tip of her nose then tenderly planted one on her lips. "Love isn't that fleeting, baby."

She frowned as she pondered what he'd just said. "I guess so. I see myself standing on the edge, afraid to dive in with you but knowing there's no other way out."

"You can trust me," he said.

She stiffened. Of course he knew that was what she needed to hear. He had always known her better than she knew herself. "Okay," she said breathlessly.

Dexter flipped her onto her back. She could feel his nectar pouring out of her. Then she felt the wet heat of his tongue mixed with the softness of his lips as his mouth worked its way down her neck. He bit and sucked one nipple into his mouth then the other as his fingers shifted in and out of her.

"Damn, I really unleashed inside you," he said.

She chuckled. "Yes, you did."

"I was overexcited." Dexter continued kissing, licking, and nibbling his way down her sternum, stomach, and pubic bone until his soft, warm tongue rounded her clit.

Robin closed her eyes and moaned as he found the spot he wanted to taste first. His stimulation made her instantly clench the bedsheets as she sucked air and cried out to the Almighty.

CHAPTER 19

*P*ain coursed through Robin's uterus. Rachel, her doula, had told her it would be hard to ignore but that she should try focusing on the beautiful things that had gotten her to that very moment.

She remembered the moment she and Dexter had made Noel, which would be their son's name. It was the day after he'd found her in the woods. They made love for the rest of the day. The servants brought them food and drinks, but they didn't come out of the room, not even after their guests arrived. They couldn't leave each other's body. Dexter was like a drug she didn't want to quit, and apparently, he felt the same.

But the next day, everyone gathered together for

lunch. The president and first lady's truth-telling mission had been deemed a minor success. Jay Harrison had had an epiphany right in the middle of his press conference and had decided to concede the presidency to his vice president and best friend, Dale Maxwell. The media was having a feeding frenzy with Ray's unexpected action. Of course quitting was never easy, but Ray Harrison was at peace with his decision. He met his granddaughters on that day.

Robin also got to know Mariana and Maribel better. They all had a really fantastic time talking politics and family. Cherry had rented a horse and buggy and gave everyone a tour of the apple orchards. Robin reflected on how happy the girls had been to see her and Dexter kiss under the twigs of the winter-worn apple trees.

Later that night as they all congregated in the den, Cherry played jazz tunes on the piano and Gran sang along with her. Amy sat close to Robin and proclaimed how lucky she was to be the woman Dexter Frampton couldn't ignore.

"Believe me, I've tried to get him to fuck me from here to Timbuktu." Her gaze softened at Dexter, who was across the room, engaged in conversation with Jay West. "He cared about me too much. He's one of the few good guys. Congratulations, Robin."

Congratulations was a little much, but Robin smiled graciously. "Thanks, Amy."

"No, really, congratulations."

Robin frowned dubiously.

Amy grinned. "I have a sixth sense about certain things, and you're pregnant."

Robin felt her eyes bulge out of her head.

"You're having a boy."

She hadn't taken Amy seriously. Robin had always believed sixth senses were no more than a person's intuitive defense mechanism.

It hadn't been until the day Soulscape Parts One, Two, and Three, which she'd added later, were shown to the public that she discovered Amy was right. After missing two periods, Robin had gone to the doctor, who'd confirmed that she was pregnant.

Another contraction stabbed her uterus, and Robin screamed to high heaven.

"Breathe, babe," Dexter said, holding her hand.

She'd heard so many stories about women not wanting their husbands in the delivery room with them. With all the dizzying pain she felt, including her hoo-ha being on fire from the final stages of stretching, she found a moment to gaze at her beautiful new husband.

Robin took a deep breath as she remembered how they'd made love on every nook and cranny while attending Jacques Blanchard's birthday party at his vineyard in Bordeaux, France. She and Dexter hadn't been able to keep their hands off each other.

When the next torturous contraction hit her less than a minute later as Dexter was counting the seconds, she pushed her mind to reflect on their wedding day.

It had been a small gathering of only family and about twenty friends, which were comprised only of the Lord family, at Harrison Orchard Estate. The apples were in bloom, and so was Robin's belly. Neither she nor Dexter could stop crying or kissing during the ceremony. Robin didn't have an ounce of fear that Dexter would ever abandon her or Noel, and that made her so happy and so in love with him that she almost fainted.

Amy told her after the ceremony that their son would be a Leo and that one day, he would be president of the United States. "My sixth sense has become sharper than ever since I got out of rehab and started studying for my degree in psychology."

Robin smiled and patronizingly said, "Thanks, Amy."

Amy winked at her. "You don't believe me, but it's going to happen."

Never, Robin thought. Even though she loved Raymond Harrison, who had been urged by a letter with seventy million signatures to finish his term as president, she still loathed politicians in general.

"Don't worry, Robin," Amy assured her. "By then, all the big money will be taken out of politics, and he'll be able to look after the interests of the people."

Now Robin knew Amy's sixth sense was going haywire. "Well, that will mean we're living in a utopia."

Amy had shrugged indifferently. "I don't know about that, but Noel Frampton-Harrison is going to be one of the best presidents this country's ever had, and how can he not be with you and Dexter as his parents."

And now the agony was such that all Robin could concentrate on was how much it hurt. Breathing wasn't working. She wanted to smack Rachel for talking her into natural childbirth.

"Do you want the drugs, baby?" Dexter yelled

as she gritted her teeth and made some noise that sounded demonic.

"No!" Robin roared. She'd come this far; she might as well go all the way.

What happened next was a painful, emotional, hellish roller coaster. She pushed when the doctor told her to. It all felt like a form of medieval torture.

"Push!"

She did.

Then she heard him cry. Noel was new to the world.

Dexter kissed her on the forehead. "Good job."

And even while her vagina was still on fire, she laughed, cried, and thanked God for the life that had been put in her and her husband's hands to love, guide, and make into a wonderful man from that day forward.

THE END

THE DARK CHRISTMASES

Intrigued (Book 1)

Desire (Book 2)

Claimed (Book 3)

ROMANTIC SUSPENSE SERIES

THE STERLINGS

Secrets & Chance, **Book 1**

Revelations, **Book 2**

Forever and Ever, **Book 3**

The Secret Keeper, **Book 4**

PARANORMAL ROMANCE SERIES

PARCHED

Parched **Book 1**

The Seventh Sister